A SIMPLE COUNTRY MYSTERY

BLYTHE BAKER

~

Death comes unexpectedly ...

With the suspicious death of a young woman in the village, Helen Lightholder finds herself once again delving into the menacing shadows that lurk beneath the pleasant surface of sunny Bookminster. Her search for suspects and motives leads her to a prisoner of war camp on the outskirts of the village, but could the real danger lie even closer to home?

Meanwhile, two very different men vie for Helen's heart, but neither can take the place of the husband she lost. As a series of break-ins leave her feeling unsafe in her home and shop, Helen has to decide whether or not to continue in the "quiet" life she has found in the country.

~

1

It was dark. So dark that I couldn't tell if my eyes were open or shut. If I blinked, it didn't seem to matter.

A chill hung in the air, as if I'd been thrust inside an icebox, and it was stagnant as I breathed in deeply through my nostrils. When I reached out with my hands, I expected my fingertips to graze against a frozen metal wall, yet found nothing more than the frigid, open air.

Where am I?

A voice somewhere broke the silence, followed by a tired sounding engine. I turned my head in the direction of the noise, and found a narrow beam of light peeking through what appeared to be a crack in a doorway.

I inched toward it, my heart hammering in my chest. My footsteps made no sound, and as I approached the light streaming in, I heard the voice again.

"This blasted tractor..." said a man in a ragged tone. "I'll never get it to work now. That foolish girl lost me the best mechanic in town."

I blinked, leaning closer to the crack.

"We should have left when we had the chance. Now I'll be carted off to prison, and the harvest will all go to waste, anyway."

I found that there was a garage on the other side, though it was far larger than any garage I had ever seen, more like a hangar. A tractor, entirely rusted through, sat outside the large door, backdropped by swaying, golden wheat just ready to be picked.

The man I'd heard stood with his back to me, surveying the tractor, his hands planted firmly on his hips. A hunting rifle hung across his back, the barrel smoking slightly.

My stomach dropped as I recognized him.

Mr. Cooke?

As if I'd called him by name, the ornery, sickly looking man glanced over his shoulder, his eyes falling directly on the narrow crack of the door.

"You!" he shouted, his brow furrowing as he turned around. "This is all your fault! If only you'd let well enough alone, I would still be – "

His voice, along with the narrow crack in the doorway, completely faded as I staggered backward.

I gasped, spinning around once again, plunged back into complete darkness.

Mr. Cooke was in prison, I reassured myself. *For killing the Polish refugee that wandered into Brookminster looking for his wife...*

For a moment, all I could hear was the sound of my own breathing, which seemed to echo in the blackness.

"...in business when I already am?" came another voice, distant once again, just barely audible through the dark. "...to think that I wouldn't retaliate in some..."

I took a hesitant step toward the voice. Once again, my footsteps made no sound.

"...thought for certain that I'd won, finally. There was no one to stand in my..."

I squinted through the shadows, trying to find another crack of light, yet this time, I found nothing.

Footsteps suddenly sounded over my head, directly above me, the sharp *clack* of heels against a polished wood floor.

"Yes, yes, I hear you," said the voice, much clearer now. I could tell it belonged to a woman...and a woman who was familiar to me. "I have them ready for you. All you need is to come and retrieve them."

The woman began to pace once again, her footfalls like fingertips drumming on a glass table.

"But Mrs. Warren, you were the one who was so eager to have more rationing coupons," the woman's voice said, and I could easily imagine a sly, curling smile on her face. "You said yourself that there was no way a woman should have to live off such stingy clothing rations as what the government has forced on us, yes?"

I frowned as I recognized the snickering tone.

It was Mrs. Martin, the woman who owned the clothing store on the other side of town...and the person who murdered my Aunt Vivian.

"Very good, dear. They are here when you're ready to pick them up. The price? Oh, come now, dear, you must know these won't come cheap. Cloth is scarce, as are those pretty shoes you were eyeing when you were in here last Tuesday."

Manipulative and deceiving...just like I remembered her being.

*Wait just a moment...*I thought. *Mrs. Martin...she isn't alive anymore. Sidney Mason – he shot her when she was trying to come after me.*

Once again, it was as if I had spoken my thoughts aloud.

"Who's there?" Mrs. Martin snapped. "Vivian, if that's you, I swear I'll – "

But her voice and her hammering footsteps were gone like a mist in the morning sun...and it was silent once again.

What in the world is happening? I asked, pressing my hands against my head. *Why are these people –*

But the thought died away in my mind as I found myself standing in a gloomy office. The sound of car horns honking greeted me, as well as the warm glow of street lamps spilling in through a long row of windows, revealing a tightly packed line of buildings across the street, bathed in the shadow of night.

I was in London.

Someone cleared his throat, drawing my attention back into the room.

Two men were hovering over a desk. The balding man who stood on one side had a cigar clamped between his teeth, the smoke billowing into the air above his head. The other...was my late husband Roger.

"Are you certain there is no other way?" asked the man with the cigar, skillfully keeping the cigar in his mouth while speaking around it.

"I'm certain," said Roger, and the sound of his voice made my heart catch in my throat.

All I could do was stare at him. How long had it been since I'd seen his face? Seven months now? Almost eight?

I'd almost forgotten his profile, his sharp jawline, strong chin, and high cheekbones. His eyes, a deep blue, regarded the man standing across from him with mingled respect and worry.

I took a step forward, longing to run to him, but I found I could not move.

"You know what this will mean, don't you?" the man asked, regret clear in his gaze.

Roger's jaw became tight, and he swallowed hard. "I do," he said. "But there's no other way."

No other way? I thought. *What does he mean by that?*

I reached out toward him, opening my mouth to shout out his name...but as soon as it left my lips, there was a sharp crack of thunder and a flash of bright lightning, so bright that I had to flinch away from the windows.

When I opened my eyes a moment later, blinking again in the sudden darkness, both Roger and the man with the cigar were gone.

My heart began to race, hammering against my ribcage like a caged bird.

Roger! I called with my mind. *Roger, where are you?*

I turned and ran from the room, out into a long, seemingly endless hallway lined with doors along one wall and windows looking out onto the streets of London on the other. I started down it, calling out to Roger.

"Roger!" I shouted, running, yet never seeming to get any closer to the other end of the hall. "Roger, where are you?"

A man suddenly appeared out of one of the doorways, dressed in a clean cut military uniform.

I staggered to a stop in front of him. "Sir, please...have you seen my husband? Roger?"

As I stared up at the man, I realized that he had no face; he was entirely hidden in shadow.

Fear gripped my heart, and I continued down the hall.

I ran into a few others like the military man, all of whom had no faces, and no voices.

Infuriated that no one would help me, or even seemed to want to try, I kept running.

Just as I thought I might never reach the end, I slammed into a wooden door, the frosted glass with the word *Investigator* etched across its surface trembling slightly.

I pushed open the door and found Roger standing in the room, staring at the opposite wall. His hands hung at his side, as if in defeat.

"Roger?" I called, my voice loud and strong.

Roger's back stiffened, and slowly, ever so slowly, he began to turn around.

My heart beat faster, eagerly waiting, longing to see him look at me once again, after so long.

But just before he turned fully, the sound of explosions in the distance, followed by flashes of light, told me I was too late.

The bombs were falling...and he was gone.

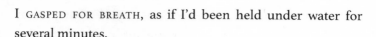

I GASPED FOR BREATH, as if I'd been held under water for several minutes.

Sitting straight up, I grabbed at my heart and my head. I checked my legs, and accounted for both of my arms, and each finger and toe.

It took the moment of blind panic to pass before I realized that I was alone, in my bedroom...having woken from a terrible nightmare.

I shuddered, wrapping my arms tightly around myself in the dark.

It was just a dream, I told myself. *Nothing more than a nightmare.*

I sat in the silence, the blood rushing through my ears for a moment or two. It was difficult to calm down as the darkness continued to press itself against me.

I turned on the light beside my bed, and my heart skipped. I was half expecting to see Mr. Cooke standing in the corner with his rifle pointed at me, or to see the body of Mrs. Martin splayed out with a fresh wound in her chest.

Neither was there. I really was alone.

Well, I'm certainly not getting back to sleep after all that... I thought.

I drew myself out of bed, sliding my feet into my slippers. In the washroom, splashing my face with warm water helped to thaw my chilled fingertips.

I glanced at the clock on my side table as I returned to the bedroom, and saw it was nearly five in the morning.

With a heavy sigh, I headed out toward the living areas.

I found a seat on the sofa after making a hot cup of tea, and sat down, my legs curled up underneath me as I tried as best I could to fight the images in my mind. It was deeply troubling that the hardest things I'd experienced in the last few months were the memories that were following me so closely, plaguing me even in my dreams where I hoped to find relief from the fears.

Mr. Cooke was behind bars now. Sam Graves, the local police inspector, had informed me of this himself. And Mrs. Martin was long dead, having been killed in my presence.

But Roger...

Instead of fighting that part of the dream, I reflected on

it for some time. As the minutes ticked by, and the sun began to rise outside the window, I thought of Roger's face, of the secrets I never learned the answers to, and the infuriating way that no one seemed to want to help.

For a moment, it was as if I'd just received the call about his passing. My chest was heavy, as if my heart had physically broken. And now just as then, I had no answers. There was no one I could call, no one who would respond to my letters. I wasn't even sure if anyone who had been with him had survived the blast. It was possible there was no one left alive who would ever know exactly what had happened to him in the first place.

My desire for answers had never left me, but it surprised me just how strongly I still felt that way.

The dream itself had felt so real, even though as I thought through it, I could easily see where it had been nothing more than a product of my own imagination. It left me feeling raw, and rather exposed.

Was that at all like what Roger was doing when he died? I wondered, the warmth from my teacup seeping into my cold, numb fingers. *Was he planning? Was he awake? Was he happy?*

Those were dangerous questions to ask, I knew. But I couldn't help it. Especially not after that sort of nightmare.

As I heard my alarm sound in the bedroom, I realized it was time to put aside the dream and begin my day. I wasn't reluctant to do so; in fact, I was relieved at the idea of doing something entirely mundane and normal. I longed for simplicity, for the physical reminders that my dream was not real, and that the waking world was.

I realized, though, that trying to distance myself from Roger's memory was not serving me well. In fact, the intentional attempt to smother those memories was only making the dreams I had worse and worse, for this was not the first nightmare I'd endured in the last few weeks. It just seemed to be one of the many.

To resolve that, I made my way up into the attic, making a beeline straight for the box that I'd so sadly put away. Roger's memory didn't deserve to be forgotten. If it was going to take me more time to heal than I had thought, then so be it.

I pulled out a picture frame that I'd hung on the wall in the room in my parents' home when he and I were living apart. We'd had it taken on our honeymoon in Italy before the war broke out. The glass inside the frame was still intact, thankfully. I'd half expected to find it shattered in my careless attempt to hide it from myself.

I also found a number of Roger's letters, all tucked away inside the box I'd purchased specifically for them, with a pretty rose carved into the top, and a little, gold lock on the front. Perhaps a bit juvenile, but I'd loved how romantic and simple it was.

I carried the things down the stairs as gently as I would have carried a sleeping child, affectionately holding them against my chest.

I set the photograph down on the mantle above the fireplace, where I could see it from everywhere in the room, and then carried the box of letters into the bedroom, where I slipped them inside the drawer of my side table until I could find a better place for them to live. As I didn't have many of Roger's earthly possessions, I wanted to eventually find a way to display these letters and honor him in a tasteful way.

As I dressed and ate a small breakfast, I found myself

much happier now that Roger's things had been taken out of that box. It was as if I'd freed myself of the guilt of hiding his belongings away, like I'd done something wrong in the first place.

It was just before seven when I made my way down the stairs to the haberdashery shop that had once belonged to my aunt. Everything was just as I'd left it the day before, ready and waiting for the customers who would inevitably come in, looking for their orders or for new ways to mend their clothing. I'd had a great deal of success at selling some clothing I'd mended myself, with new collars, buttons, and hems.

But before I was to start my day, I had made plans to enjoy some tea and biscuits with my dear friend, Irene Driscoll.

As I stepped outside into the cool, morning mist, I took a deep breath. The air smelled of freshly cut grass and the wet earth; it must have rained in the night. The flowers in my front garden were in full bloom, giving the walk a friendly, inviting feel.

It wasn't long before I saw Irene making her way up High Street toward my little cottage, wearing a lovely pink parka with large, black buttons.

She lifted her hand in a wave as she approached, and I did the same in return.

"Good morning," I said, smiling at her. The nightmare was finally starting to lose its grip on my heart.

"Well, good morning," Irene said, a grin spreading across her pretty, round face. Her blonde hair was pulled back in a braid that circled her head like a crown. "I think we might be in for some more rain this morning. I'm certain the teahouse will be quite busy today."

"This summer has been good for business, hasn't it?" I asked, opening the front gate for her.

A movement out of the corner of my eye caught my attention, and I looked up to see Sidney Mason, the handsome man who lived next door, coming toward us.

"Good morning to you, sir," I said, waving at him.

As he lifted his ginger head, though, my heart sank.

Something was wrong.

"Hello, ladies," he said in his Scottish accent, coming to a stop beside us. He adjusted the dark fedora he wore, worry written all over his handsome, freckled face.

"Whatever is the matter, Mr. Mason?" Irene asked from beside me. "You look positively dreadful this morning."

He heaved a deep sigh, scratching the back of his neck. "I certainly wish I'd woken up to better news," he said. "Have either of you read the paper yet?"

Irene and I glanced at one another. "No, not yet," I said.

"Neither have I," Irene said. "Nathanial always fetches it on his way out in the mornings."

"What happened?" I asked, my heart racing. "Is it something to do with the war?"

He shook his head. "No, not this time…"

He looked at me, his piercing gaze cutting right through me.

"There was another murder in town," he said. "Just two days ago."

2

"**A**nother *murder?*" Irene asked, incredulous, her jaw hanging open. "You cannot be serious."

Sidney nodded. "I certainly wish I was not," he said. "Unfortunately, the news was confirmed by Mr. Hodgins this morning."

Mr. Hodgins, the town butcher, was always up before the sunrise to prepare his shop for the day. I had never known a butcher who kept his produce as fresh as he did, and from what his wife had told me, he wasted hardly anything.

"What exactly did he say?" Irene asked, her brow furrowing.

"Just what the newspaper reported," Sidney said.

I turned around and glanced at the welcome mat near my front door. Lying there, half in a puddle, was my own morning paper.

I hurried to it and snatched it from the water, the edges of the page dripping as I carried it back toward the garden gate.

"It should be right there on the front page," Sidney said, pointing at the paper in my hands.

I unfolded the sopping paper, the ink bleeding through and making it difficult to read. After peeling some of the pages apart, I scanned the headlines.

War Entering Tense Times!

Rationing Restrictions Reevaluated!

Tired of Tuesdays? Try Tommy's Time Wasters!

"I don't see it," I said, looking up at Sidney.

"Down there, toward the bottom," he said.

Irene leaned over my shoulder as I flipped the paper over and found a small column in the bottom corner, written in tiny font that was rather difficult to read.

"Woman found dead in her home; Police suspect foul play."

I stared up at Irene, my mouth hanging open slightly.

"How dreadful..." Irene said, laying a hand over her heart. "Does it say who it was?"

I returned my gaze to the page, my eyes searching through the words.

"Mrs. Lowell, a local widow, was found dead early Monday morning in her home by her daughter..." I read.

"Mrs. Lowell?" Irene asked, and her face fell. "Oh, my word..."

"Who is Mrs. Lowell?" I asked. "I'm not sure I've ever met her."

Irene rested her palm against her cheek. "She was perhaps the sweetest woman in this whole village. A fantastic painter with such a gentle heart, an artist, through and through."

"Was she the petite woman with the blonde hair?" Sidney asked. "The one who always hung around the park on Ivy Street?"

"The same," Irene said. "Her daughter, Evangeline, is the spitting image of her, as well...and good heavens, she can't be any older than Michael is...ten at the very oldest."

My heart ached for the poor girl, as well as for the mother.

"What else does it say?" Irene asked, eyeing the paper in my hands.

I returned my gaze to it, clearing my throat. *"When the police arrived, she was unresponsive. She was rushed to the hospital, where she spent several hours under careful observation of the doctors, but was pronounced dead at 12:04 pm."*

"But how?" Irene asked. "How did this poor woman die?"

Sidney sighed, his hands on his hips. "The article doesn't explain," he said. "But as the headline says, the police suspect violence."

Irene frowned. "I just hope that poor girl didn't find her mother in some bloody mess...it must have been troubling enough to find her in the first place."

Sidney shook his head. "When I spoke with Mr. Hodgins this morning, he seemed to think that it might have been a poisoning, or perhaps something as simple as a heart attack," he said. "He seemed to think that the reports were far too eager to paint this as a murder as opposed to just a natural death."

I gave Sidney a searching look. "What do you think?" I asked.

He shrugged. "How can I know? I haven't seen the body, and goodness knows if it was some sort of gruesome murder, no one else will, either, as they will certainly have a closed casket funeral..."

"Well, it seems they wished to keep this quiet until the

police were ready to discuss it," Irene said, holding out her hand for the paper. "May I?"

I nodded, passing it to her, feeling rather hollow inside.

Her eyes scanned the page, and she picked up where I left off. "*Inspector Graves was pulled aside for questioning at the scene; 'We would like to assure everyone that the matter has been handled, and that Mrs. Lowell's daughter is going to be taken to a foster home where she will be cared for until we can find a family to take her in.'*"

Irene shook her head. "A foster home? As far as I know, Mrs. Lowell had no family in the village anywhere. She and her husband moved here when they were married some years ago, and she couldn't have been older than eighteen at the time."

So...this woman was likely younger than I was...and she was already dead?

"That's awfully young to die like she did," Sidney said, folding his arms and echoing my thoughts almost exactly. With a glance at him, a chill ran down my spine. "She couldn't have even been thirty then, right?"

"Precisely," Irene said sadly. "She lost her husband in the war last year, and has been struggling to make ends meet since then."

"And they're just going to put her daughter in a foster home? Just like that?" I asked.

"Well, it's probably to keep her safe for now," Sidney said. "What else should they do?"

I hesitated. "I don't know, but she just lost her mother, and now she has to go and live with an entirely new family?"

"It's better than living in that house all on her own," Irene said. "Sam Graves will ensure her safety, I'm certain."

"Yes, of course," Sidney said, nodding in agreement. "The authorities will make sure she is taken care of."

He stared up the street, and then glanced at his watch.

"I am terribly sorry to be the bearer of such bad news today, ladies," he said. "And I'm also sorry that it is all I have time to discuss today. Unfortunately, I have a job I must get to this morning."

"That's quite all right," I said. "You go on. Irene, do you still want to stay for tea?"

"Yes, I could certainly use it after all that." She waved at Sidney. "Goodbye, Mr. Mason. As unfortunate as the news you brought us was, I'm certainly glad we were able to discuss it with someone. I'm sure it will be on everyone's mind come this afternoon. It will help me be better prepared when I open the teahouse."

"My pleasure, Irene," Sidney said. His blue eyes moved onto me, and I felt a shiver as a small smile tugged at the corner of his lips. "And you have a good day too...all right, Helen?"

My face flushed with color, but I nodded and returned the smile. "Thank you," I said. "You as well."

With that, he started back toward his house, where I saw his car parked in the front drive.

"Come on, dear," Irene said, wrapping her arms tightly around herself. "Let's get in out of this drizzling mist."

The ends of my hair were clinging to my blouse and shoulders as we stepped back inside, and my skin, slick with the fine rain, glistened as I flicked on the lights in the shop.

~

THE TEA DIDN'T TAKE LONG to heat. Soon we both cradled the warm, steaming cups in our hands.

"I just can't stop thinking about poor Mrs. Lowell," Irene said, shaking her head. "She's had it so rough the last few years, and now to find out that she passed away in the prime of her life? It's just too much to take in."

I stared down into my tea, the sugar still melting in the hot liquid. "I cannot help but feel connected to this woman," I said. "Not only did she pack up and move to this small village, but she also lost her husband to the war..."

Irene sighed heavily. "I should have introduced the two of you. I imagine it would have been nice for her to have a friend who would understand what she's been going through. It really helps to put things into perspective, doesn't it? Life can be over in the blink of an eye...and far too often it happens too soon."

My throat grew tight. The nightmares I had endured the night before now felt like child's play in comparison to the news of yet another death in the village.

"How do you think her daughter is going to handle this?" I asked quietly.

"I can't imagine very well," Irene answered, frowning. "Especially if she was the one to find Abigail."

The images that flooded my mind in that moment were rather gruesome; a woman sprawled out across the kitchen floor, breakfast half finished on the counter. The same woman sitting upright in her favorite chair, her eyes wide and staring, her head lolling to the side. And an even worse scenario, where the poor girl wandered into her mother's bedroom, only to see her mother's hand outstretched on the floor, streaked with blood...not moving.

I shuddered, shaking the pictures from my mind.

"I hope they will be able to find family for her to go to," I said. "People who will take care of her, love her and help her get through this."

"As do I," Irene said. "You know, I find it all rather strange how these sorts of things keep happening in Brookminster. For as long as I can remember, this used to be such a quiet place, where hardly anything exciting ever happened. I should know, my brother likes to mention it every time he comes to visit."

"I was thinking the same thing," I said. "If I was a superstitious woman, I would believe I brought my own bad luck with me when I moved here."

Irene pursed her lips, shaking her head. "That's nonsense, dear, and you know that. These things happen, and from what I know, they often come in waves. What's the old saying...death comes in threes?"

"Then let's hope this is the end of them," I said, frowning.

I felt Irene's gaze on me, and when I looked at her, I found her expression hard and serious.

"What's the matter?" I asked, setting down my teacup.

"You know very well what I'm thinking," Irene said. "If you feel like you're responsible for these deaths, then I know you well enough now to know that you will want to get involved so you can get to the bottom of it and figure out what happened."

"I don't know what you're talking about," I said, averting my gaze, my cheeks flooding with color. "I have no interest in getting involved. Besides, I didn't even know Mrs. Lowell."

"No, but you told me that you already feel connected to her, given your similar situations," Irene said. She sighed. "Please promise me you will just go about your life, dear.

The last thing I want is for you to get hurt, or find yourself in yet another dangerous situation."

"I know," I said. "I understand. And I appreciate your concern for me, Irene. I really do."

Irene's gaze seemed suspicious, and I knew she was as well aware as I was that I had not, in fact, promised not to get involved at all.

The truth was that I had already, in a way, promised myself that after I was done with work that day, I intended to do some more digging into this woman's death.

After all, if someone is now coming after widows, then how can I be sure that I won't be next?

3

Everything went smoothly in the shop that day. Customers came by, modifying or picking up their orders. I somehow managed to stay on top of them all, having developed a rather clever organization system that Sidney himself had helped me with, with individual drawers labeled with the different customers' names.

I managed to organize an entire shipment of buttons that had come in nearly every color, all thrown into a box from the place where I'd ordered them second hand. Hundreds of buttons all needed to be sorted and placed in with their matches of the same shade and shape.

When three o'clock came around, I was quite ready to be done for the day. It seemed that nearly every customer who walked through my door had something to say about Mrs. Lowell's death.

Even though we had all read the same article, which was incredibly vague and left a great deal to the imagination, almost everyone had an opinion about what had happened.

More than that, they were speculating about who had killed the poor woman in the first place.

"Must have been some jealous ex-lover," said Mrs. Georgianna to a friend of hers when they stepped up to pay for their new hats. "Why else would they have moved to a place where they didn't know a soul all those years ago?"

Other customers had different ideas.

"What if it was little Evangeline?" asked Mrs. Diggory in a hushed tone to her husband. "She's always been so very quiet...I've been worried about the boys spending any time with her. She's always had that distant look...don't you think? And who would suspect a child?"

But none of these theories were as ridiculous as what I'd heard from Mrs. Wells, the wife of one of the police officers who worked for Sam Graves.

"You know, my husband has it on good authority that she was killed by the Germans," she said to me, her eyes wide as she passed me her money across the counter. "He thinks they're afraid her soldier husband told her things that were confidential, and they sent a spy to silence her."

I didn't commit to any sort of response to her, but realized that Mrs. Wells was also notorious for believing her garden hose to be haunted, and that she could communicate with her St. Bernard, Louie.

"All I'm saying is that we should all remain vigilant," she said in a harsh whisper as I passed her a small hat box wrapped in blue ribbon. "Spies could be anywhere... anyone. We can't ever be too careful."

"Of course, Mrs. Wells. I'll do my best to stay alert," I said.

She nodded sharply, taking her box and hurrying from the store.

After closing the shop, I changed out of my working clothes and into something a little better for going out in. Not only did I have errands of my own to run, but I felt a very strong pull to remain in the sway of the gossip around town. And the only way for me to do that was to follow after it, and keep my finger on the pulse of this story.

Sidney had mentioned Mr. Hodgins, the butcher. It seemed he was familiar with the story. And knowing him, his shop would likely be very busy, especially this close to suppertime.

I quickly changed, brushed my teeth, and splashed some cool water on my flushed face.

As I dabbed at my cheeks with the towel, I met my own stare in the mirror, and for the first time in what felt like months, I really looked at myself.

My hair was the same as it always was; long, straight, the color of deeply steeped tea. It was getting a little long, though...it might have been time to get a trim.

My eyes were the same steely blue that I'd seen every day since I was born.

And I seemed so thin...I could clearly see the bones in my wrists, and my cheeks seemed somewhat sunken in.

I touched my face, felt my jaw, which protruded more than it used to.

The truth was, I hardly recognized myself anymore. At least, I didn't recognize the look in my eyes, the somewhat lost, and haunted expression.

I had known that Roger's death had taken its toll on me. I'd noticed it less than others, like my mother who often telephoned and reminded me to eat more than I normally would want to, or Irene who was always sending me home with little tea cakes and biscuits and sweets, just to make me happy.

The pain was clear in my eyes, though. I couldn't even hide it from myself.

I tried to force a smile, but it seemed utterly fake, and it only made my heart ache instead.

It wasn't just pain that was evident. There was a hardness in my gaze now, too.

I'd experienced death, stared it in the face more than once, since moving to Brookminster. Those were the sorts of things that either made or broke people, weren't they?

If I was honest with myself, I wasn't quite sure which it had done to me...

For the very first time since coming to Brookminster, I wondered if I had made the right decision to move here in the first place.

Did I make the decision too hastily? Should I have given myself more of a chance to heal, surrounded by those who loved me and wanted to take care of me?

Coming here was meant to be my way of healing, of moving on from the past, I thought. *But it's never that easy, is it? Distance alone is not going to be enough to cure my heartache.*

I knew it was best not to wallow in self-pity, especially after the sort of day I'd had.

I'm just tired, I assured myself. *After those horrible dreams, and then finding about Mrs. Lowell. I just need a good night's rest, and I'll feel much better after I get to sleep.*

But sleep was going to have to wait until a more reasonable time. For now, I thought it would be best if I learned about this poor Mrs. Lowell's death...and perhaps what might have caused the killer to go after her in particular, in hopes that I might discern if other women like me, widowed or living alone, were in danger at all.

I made my way down the street to the butcher's shop, my rationing coupons tucked inside my purse. There were several people wandering to and fro down the streets, enjoying the break of the rain that day. The clouds were blocking most of the sun, keeping the heat of July at bay, but it still surprised me that it was as humid out as it was.

The butcher's shop had the door thrown open, which was strange, given his tendency to keep fresh meat out on the counter, weighing and measuring it for customers as they streamed in through the doorway. I thought that he would have detested the possibility of flies, or other such creatures.

As I stepped inside, though, I realized the open door was not purely for the temperature, but to account for all of the people that were waiting inside.

They were packed like sardines. I saw hands in the air, waving tickets. I heard a voice call out a number from behind the counter, only to realize that it was Gary Hodgins, Mr. Hodgin's oldest son. He wore the same white apron as his father, and he peered down from behind the counter for the hand that corresponded with his number.

I moved inside, the scent of sweat and raw meat hanging in the humid air. Having the door open was clearly meant to keep the temperature inside the small storefront down.

"Hodgins, I've been waiting here for almost an hour!" called an elderly gentleman with a taupe fedora on, scowling from beside a rack of spices and packaged jerky.

"Order number seventeen!" yelled Gary, cupping his hand over his mouth. "Order number seventeen, you're up next!"

There was a clear protest from some of the customers, and the densely packed group standing shoulder to shoulder all began to move as one toward the counter.

"Now, now, you all are going to have to wait your turn," Mr. Hodgins said from the counter, waving his large butcher's blade toward the crowd, his brow furrowing. His bald head glistened in the heat, and I was secretly grateful that I would not be ordering any chicken that day, as the one splayed out beneath him might have caught more than a drop or two of his perspiration. "And just so you all know, we are just about out of the spicy sausage."

"But that's my order!" called another customer. "And I'm not up until number twenty-one!"

"Eighteen!" Gary yelled over the people. "Eighteen, you're up next!"

The group shifted toward the front again, the voices of all the customers trying to talk over one another, echoing off the walls of the small room.

"...and I couldn't believe it when I saw it, right there, in black and white this morning," I heard a woman to the left of me say to the woman she was standing with. "Abigail Lowell...dead."

I froze, clutching my rationing tickets to my chest as the man beside me blew his nose into a handkerchief, a wet and nasty sound.

"I could hardly believe it myself," said her friend, who wore a pretty pink hat with netting that rested over her face. "I half expected her to sell her house, or have to sell some jewelry, or something of the kind. But to end up dead?"

"Oy, are you two talking about Mrs. Lowell?" It was Mr. Hodgins asking the question, his scowl firmly back in place. "I've heard nothing but her name spread around this store today. I'd kindly ask you to not dishonor the deceased with idle chatter the way you are."

"But didn't you hear, Mr. Hodgins?" said the woman with the pink hat. She leaned in closer to the counter, her gloved hands resting against the glass of the display case. "Some of us think we might know what happened to poor Mrs. Lowell."

Mr. Hodgins brought his cleaver down onto the leg of the bird, slicing it clean through. "Oh?" he asked, clearly interested despite himself. He appeared torn for a moment between good intentions and curiosity but, in the end, his curiosity won out. He asked, "And what might that be?"

The woman with the pink hat glanced back over her shoulder at her friend, a strange glint in her eye. They exchanged a knowing smile before she turned back to Mr. Hodgins.

"Well, there is a rumor that has been going around for some weeks now about Mrs. Lowell's landlady, Mrs. Douglas," said the woman.

"Mrs. Douglas?" Mr. Hodgins asked as his son called out yet another number – "Nineteen!" – glancing back and forth among the group standing around. The butcher seemed suddenly to remember his earlier resolution. "Listen, I would really appreciate it if you would keep your gossiping to a minimum – "

"Oh, but this isn't just gossip," the woman with the pink hat said. "It seems that Mrs. Lowell was having a difficult time paying her rent. That's a secret to no one."

"Everyone knows she fell on hard times after her husband passed away," Mr. Hodgins said. "But I hadn't realized things were as bad as all that for her."

"Yes, it seems that Mrs. Douglas was actually lending her

money for the last few months," the woman said, nodding eagerly.

"I fail to see the problem," Mr. Hodgins said, retrieving yet another chicken from behind himself, tucked away in an ice box. Thankfully, this one was already missing its head. I never liked chancing upon the shop when he was busy cleaving them off.

"The problem *is,* Mr. Hodgins, that Mrs. Douglas became furious with Mrs. Lowell, saying that she was taking advantage of her kindness," the woman said.

"Why on earth would Mrs. Douglas be angry with her?" Mr. Hodgins asked, exchanging his cleaver for a much more sinister looking blade, one that was long and could likely cut through the meat as easily as if it were butter. "If she was the one helping, then she had no right to be angry."

"Yes, yes, that's what we all thought, too. Mrs. Douglas doing something kind for someone else? When we'd heard, we thought her icy heart had perhaps thawed finally," the woman said. "We thought she was softening, looking after Abigail and young Evangeline like she was."

"But then she got cross," said the woman's friend, who wore glasses that were as thick as bottle glass. "So angry, in fact, that the two women had quite the row some weeks ago."

Mr. Hodgins looked suspiciously back and forth between the two women.

"I'm serious," said the bespectacled woman. "My granddaughter is very good friends with little Evangeline. Just last weekend, during my granddaughter's birthday, she was over and I overheard the two girls talking about Mrs. Douglas. It seems that Evangeline witnessed a terrible squabble between her mother and the landlady."

"You know how kids talk, though," Mr. Hodgins said, his scowl returning. "They tend to blow things out of proportion."

"Normally, I would agree with you," the woman said. "But this poor girl...you should have seen her face. She said that Mrs. Douglas yelled at her mother, saying that she would sue her and take everything she was worth, and that she didn't care that her husband was dead and gone." Her face fell, and her gaze became distant. "And then the child told us that her mother just burst into tears, and didn't stop crying for the rest of the day..."

Mr. Hodgins lobbed his knife into the foul, slicing its wing clean off. He seemed to consider her words for a few moments.

"Number twenty-one!" I heard his son call out, waving his hand in the air on the opposite side of the counter.

"Have you brought any of this to the police?" Mr. Hodgins asked. "Given the information about her death, they might find something like this interesting, maybe even helpful for their investigation."

"You read the papers; they said they already had it under control," the woman said with a dismissive wave. "If the police suspect Mrs. Douglas, I'm certain they would have already interrogated her by now and gotten whatever information they need."

"Number twenty-two!"

"Oh, that's us, Mr. Hodgins," said the woman, scuttling off to the side, smiling up at him as if they'd been discussing the weather and not some other poor woman's demise. "You have a good day, won't you? Say hello to your Annie for us."

Mr. Hodgins gave the two women a small wave as they

were reabsorbed by the crowd making their way toward Gary.

I stepped up to the counter, and grabbed a number ticket from the turnstile.

"Good afternoon, Mrs. Lightholder," Mr. Hodgins said in a rather heavy tone, slicing the breastbone of the chicken with such deftness and skill that I watched in some amazement.

"Good afternoon," I said.

"Did you overhear all that?" he asked, his gaze shifting downward along the counter to the woman in the pink hat who was picking up her purchases from Gary.

I followed his gaze, hesitating.

"It seems a bit farfetched, thinking it might have been old Mrs. Douglas..." he said. "She's always been a sour woman, but I have a hard time believing she would go so far as to..." his words died. "Well, I just cannot believe it. Not for one second. Especially when she was trying to help Mrs. Lowell in the first place."

I wasn't confident enough to respond to him, worried that any sort of statement might come back to bite me if the police decided to come and talk to Mr. Hodgins.

I picked up my purchases, handed over my rationing tickets, and hurried from the shop, the pressure of all the people inside making me lightheaded.

Mrs. Douglas. I'd heard her name around town before, especially from those at the teahouse. One thing was for certain; she did not have the best reputation around. From what I'd heard, she was rather moody, reclusive, and egotistical.

I'd never met her myself, though, and I wondered what Irene might have said about her. She always seemed to have a good head about the people in town, and always seemed to know who everyone was.

So the rumor flying around, so soon after Mrs. Lowell's death was announced, was that Mrs. Douglas had a bone to pick with the deceased. That certainly didn't look good.

These were the sorts of whispers that might have easily been missed by the police, especially if they had failed to ask the general public about Mrs. Lowell.

Was that the best place for me to start, then?

As I put away my purchases, I wondered if Irene was right about my involvement in these matters. Was I being utterly foolish by continually inserting myself in these situations?

Perhaps I was. But Mrs. Lowell was a war widow, and as I was one, then I needed to be careful...didn't I? What if someone in town was targeting single or widowed women who lived alone?

I need to find out, I thought. *As soon as I do, I can finally relax.*

...Or so I hoped.

4

I didn't waste any time. I knew I wouldn't be able to sleep if I didn't start investigating this as soon as possible.

Besides, it was better than sitting in my cottage, all alone, dwelling on the nightmares I'd had the night before. So before the sun set, I headed out into town, determined to find some answers to all these new questions I had.

I knew I had to be cautious. There were only a certain few people I could talk to that wouldn't become suspicious of me. That meant Irene was out, as was Sidney. If either of them knew I was digging into this case, I would never hear the end of it, even if I were to explain to them my fears about the same thing happening to me that had happened to the victim.

I made my way down to the village pub, knowing that some of the gentlemen there might not even remember my being there, depending on how long they had been there that day.

It was just after six when I stepped inside, the smell of

cigars and stale ale greeting me as soon as I opened the door. The lights were dim, and the low murmur of voices told me that it was just as full as it was every other night.

I recognized many of the faces as I wandered toward the bar. Men with good jobs, men with families and wives they loved. But even they struggled to face the hard times the war had brought upon this small town. It broke my heart to see that the only way some of them thought they could escape the pain was at the bottom of a tankard.

I stepped up to the bar, smiling at the bar tender who I did not recognize.

"What'll it be?" he asked in a dreary tone.

"Oh, um..." I said, looking around. "I'll just have some soda water, thank you."

He glared at me, realizing that likely meant no tip for him, but turned and made his way down the bar to make the drink.

"Well, I thought I recognized that voice..." said the man sitting on the stool beside me.

It was Mr. Georgianna, husband to Mrs. Francine Georgianna, and owner of the grocery store in town. He was a kindly man, with greying hair that was balding at a small spot on the crown of his head, which he usually hid with a hat.

"Good evening, Mr. Georgianna," I said, taking the seat beside his.

"I'm rather surprised to see you here, Mrs. Lightholder," he said. "You didn't strike me as the type who liked to kick back at the pub."

"Typically, I'm not," I said as the bartender brought me my soda water, setting the glass down hard enough to make the soda water slosh inside. "I actually came looking for information about something rather important."

There was some color in Mr. Georgianna's cheeks, but I knew that he might still very well remember my presence here, and thought it best to tread carefully.

I leaned closer to him, lowering my voice. "Did you hear about what happened to poor Mrs. Lowell?"

"Oh, I certainly did," he said in an equally quiet tone, nodding. "Tragic, that. Truly. She was such a young woman, about your age."

"Yes, it's been troubling me all day," I said, wrapping my arms around myself and pretending to suppress a shudder... even though the thought truly was rather disturbing. "I never knew the woman, or anything about her...but as you said, she was so close to my own age, and..."

"Oh, I know, dear, I know," he said, laying a gentle hand on my arm. "No need to fuss, though. You aren't in any danger. These sorts of things, they're terrible, but they happen."

"I just wish I knew if they caught the one who did it..." I said, rather pathetically. It seemed to be working on him, so I kept it up. "I'm not even certain where the poor woman lived; is it close to my own home? Are you certain I will not be in danger?"

"You live on High Street, yes?" Mr. Georgianna asked. He shook his head. "No, she lived clear on the other side of town, in that house with the blue shutters she was renting from Mrs. Douglas. It's on Kensington Avenue, I believe."

That's precisely the information I needed, I thought.

"Well...all right, then," I said, perhaps a bit childishly. "But you haven't heard anything else about it, have you? I'm worried I won't be able to sleep tonight..."

"Don't worry, lass," he said. "The police are investigating. In fact, I saw Mr. Wells this very evening, and I heard the police were knee deep in the case. They'll find the sorry bloke who did this sooner or later. So rest easy, all right? And if you're really worried about it, just have that nice Sidney Mason install some locks for you, just as an extra precaution."

"That's a brilliant idea, Mr. Georgianna," I said, smiling at him. "Oh, thank you so very much. I feel better now."

He walked me to the door soon after that and bid me farewell at the street.

I started down the road like I was heading home, but as soon as I was out of sight, I ducked into a narrow alleyway between two homes and started east toward Kensington Avenue.

This was a rather pretty part of town. There were hardly any shops, and the waterwheel that had been standing alongside the river lazily churned away in the dying light of the sun.

A park stood on the corner of Kensington and Ivy Street, one of the main thoroughfares in town. It was rather small, but had a lovely trellis with ivy and blooming flowers climbing up it, along with a stone path leading underneath. A stone fountain that must have been over a hundred years old sat in the very heart of it, bubbling and shimmering in the last golden light of the day.

I started down the street, noticing just how quiet it seemed. It was almost eerie. Mrs. Lowell hadn't been the only one to live on this street, had she?

It was lined with cottages just like my own, though smaller in scale.

As I walked, I noted the different color shutters on the

walls of the homes, ranging everywhere from white, to green, to red.

The smallest house at the end of the street had faded blue shutters that looked desperately in need of a fresh coat of paint.

The front garden was overgrown and rather wild, with weeds striking up through the bricks of the pathway, and piles of old, rotting leaves tucked in the flower beds beneath the windows.

The front door, painted red, was chipped and splintered, certainly in need of a good sanding.

I frowned as I noticed a crack in one of the windows, with billowy, white lace curtains hanging inside, yellowed slightly from the sunlight.

But it was the yellow *Caution* tape stretched across the front gate that made a chill run down my spine.

It was a poor excuse for a house, and in my anger, I wondered how Mrs. Lowell had been able to stand living there as long as she had. Why in the world had Mrs. Douglas let the house fall into such disrepair? Didn't she realize there was a child living there?

I continued down the street, hoping that people living in the other nearby homes might look out and see me as nothing more than a curious passerby.

My mind began to race as I started to form possible scenarios in my mind about what had happened a few nights before. Mrs. Douglas seemed like she could be a perfectly reasonable candidate for the murderer, just given her relationship with the victim. She knew the house and likely had a spare key to get in. They'd had a fight recently, and when money was the root of the issue, things never ended well...

I rounded on my heel at the end of the road, and started back down the street, hoping to get a glimpse of the house one more time.

As I drew closer, though, I noticed I wasn't the only one looking at the house. A rather large, broad shouldered man was standing across the street, scrawling something down in a notebook in his hand.

My heart skipped, and my face flooded with color. There was nowhere for me to hide. He was going to see me, know that it was me –

*Stay calm...*I thought. *He seems busy enough, taking notes down about the property. If I slip in through an alleyway here, walk down to the park and back onto Ivy Street, he'll never see –*

"Helen Lightholder? Is that you?"

His voice called out to me just as I was about to scurry between two other golden-stoned houses.

I winced, my breath catching in my throat.

Footsteps behind me confirmed what I'd feared.

As I turned, I found myself staring up into the face of Sam Graves, police inspector for Brookminster.

He was as handsome as he was tall, with broad shoulders and chest that matched his wide jaw and strong cheekbones. His dark hair flecked with grey was cut shorter than I'd seen him wear it before, but his gaze was still the same piercing blue that it always was.

"I thought that was you," he said in his deep, gravelly voice.

I sighed heavily. "Yes, it's me," I said. "And I know what you're about to say, so please just – "

"Oh?" he interrupted. "And what do you think I'm going to say?"

I folded my arms. "You are going to scold me for coming

out here. You are going to tell me to keep my nose out of police business, and to stay away from everything to do with this case."

Sam considered my words, pursing his lips thoughtfully. He nodded a moment later. "Not terribly far off, but I've learned that my frustration does little to dissuade you. To be honest, I'm not all that surprised to see you around here. And in a way, I'm almost glad I ran into you."

I blinked up at him. *Sam Graves is glad to have run into me?*

"So, what, then? Are you going to try and sweet talk me into staying away?" I asked.

He shook his head. "No, not at all. I've come to realize that instead of trying to shove you away, it might be in my best interest to utilize your help...if you are interested, that is."

My eyes narrowed as I regarded him carefully. "This feels like a trap," I said.

"No trap," he said. "In the past, you have proven to be surprisingly perceptive, and you have been able to root out information that the police never could, purely because of who we are and what we stand for. We frighten people. You, though? You are charismatic, and that helps others to be comfortable answering your questions."

"Are you telling me that you want me to...what? Go undercover for you?" I asked. "Isn't that breaking some sort of law, somewhere? I am just a civilian, after all."

He studied me carefully for a moment. "How would you feel about getting something to eat with me?" he asked, sliding his hands into his pockets. "My treat, of course."

It took a great deal of self control to not let my jaw hit the cobblestones beneath me.

His expression was blank, though, so I couldn't tell what he was thinking.

"That is rather unexpected coming from you," I said.

He shrugged. "Yes, well, I suppose you really only know the side of me that has to deal with murderers and thieves for a living. So, what do you say?"

Something still felt strange, but I couldn't put my finger on what it was, exactly.

"I suppose there's no harm in it..." I said.

"Good," Sam said, turning to step back out of the alleyway. "Let's get going, then."

He ended up taking me to the inn run by Mr. and Mrs. Diggory, which was somewhat quiet for the middle of the summer. The dining room had more than a few empty tables, and Mr. Diggory seemed eager for customers.

"You don't have to worry about a thing this evening, Mr. Graves," Mr. Diggory said. "I will ensure that you have the best service."

"Thank you very much, Mr. Diggory," Sam said as we found ourselves at a table beside one of the two large bay windows overlooking the front street.

Mr. Diggory smiled at me, too, a kind smile that I hadn't seen him wear, before hurrying away to fetch us some water.

"I'm confused," I said. "The last time I saw Mr. Diggory, he seemed to be an entirely different person. Devastated over the loss of his son, and really quite sour to anyone he came across."

"Yes, I was rather troubled by that change in character, as well," Sam said, his gaze following after Mr. Diggory. "But I think his behavior was turning many people away from the inn..."

I thought back to that afternoon in the cemetery, when the rain had been falling hard, and the air had a bite to it.

"I saw him paying his respects to the Polish refugee some weeks ago," I said. "I'd gone to do the same, and he told me how awful he felt for treating the deceased so poorly, just because of what had happened to his son."

"It made perfect sense to me," Sam said, his dark eyebrows knitting together. "That beggar brought more trouble on himself than necessary."

Mr. Diggory returned with some glasses of water, and a basket with a napkin folded over inside. "Freshly baked bread from the kitchens," he said, setting it down between us. "And my wife's famous garlic herb butter."

The bread smelled heavenly as he pulled aside the napkin, revealing the crusty, golden loaf beneath.

"I'll be right back with the meal," he said, hurrying off.

Sam peered at the bread, and then at me. "You go on ahead. Too much bread makes me feel sick."

"That's unfortunate," I said.

He shrugged. "Been that way since I was a kid."

I picked out a thickly cut piece, and slathered some of the garlic butter across it. "So, you were saying about the beggar?" I asked.

"Yes," Sam said, picking up his water and swirling the glass around as if it were some fine wine. "He asked for a lot of the trouble he got into. I met his daughter, you see. Found out some very interesting things about him and his past...it seems our Polish beggar was not all that innocent, after all."

With a sinking feeling in my stomach, I looked away, losing a lot of the pleasure in eating the bread. I swallowed, my mouth tasting more like sawdust now. "Not so innocent? Why do you say that?"

Sam arched an eyebrow at me before leaning forward onto the table. "Helen...why are you so interested in all these bizarre happenings in Brookminster?" he asked.

The bluntness of the question caught me completely off guard, yet suddenly I understood why he'd asked me to join him for dinner in the first place.

From the hard look in his eyes, it was clear he'd been waiting to ask me this for some time now.

I lifted my own glass of water, taking a few hesitant sips in order to collect my thoughts. That was rather difficult to do underneath his scrutinizing stare.

I decided the truth was best, in the end.

I brushed some hair from my eyes. "All of these cases... these deaths that have happened since my arrival...they've all moved me in some way," I said. "The first one I had absolutely no interest in getting involved with. If anything, I was terrified. The idea that someone had killed my own aunt, it was almost too much to bear. But I knew that if I was to ever sleep another night underneath that roof, I needed to know the truth. And so I dug and dug until I learned everything... and I'm quite glad I did."

Sam folded his arms, his eyes narrowing as he listened. "Go on," he said.

I swallowed hard, not having the courage to look away. "With the beggar, I felt tied to him because Sidney Mason and I had met him when he arrived in town – "

"Yes, I know all this," Sam said, waving me on. "That doesn't explain why you felt the need to find his killer, though."

"He had no one, as far as I could tell. He needed help, and I know what that's like. It was clear he was desperate, and after learning that he was looking for his wife, I knew that – "

Sam's eyes narrowed even further. "How did you know he was looking for his wife?"

It was as if I'd swallowed my tongue. There was no way I could have known that information unless I'd overheard the conversation he'd had with the dead man's daughter.

Sam shook his head, leaning back in his chair. And to my surprise, *he laughed.*

"I should have known the waitress at the teahouse that day was you," he said. "Who else would have taken nearly five minutes to clear a table?"

My face flooded with color. "I'm sorry. I realize that I was in the wrong, and I should have respected both yours and the family's privacy, but I – "

"It's all right," Sam said, still chuckling somewhat. "I should just expect you to show up at the scene of the crime from now on...which was why I wasn't all that surprised to see you tonight. So...tell me what it is about this case that has you so interested?"

"Well..." I said. "It's because I feel like I had things in common with Mrs. Lowell. She wasn't much younger than I am, and she lost her husband to the war...just like I did."

Sam's smile fell, and he cleared his throat, sitting up a little straighter. "I...had forgotten you two had that in common. My deepest condolences."

I folded my arms, my face burning as I stared down at the table. "It's...well, it is what it is. And so I wanted to understand this case because...well, I feel a certain kinship with the woman. And anyway, what if she was killed by someone targeting widows or women living alone? Women like me?"

"That's possible, I suppose," Sam said. "But don't you think it's a bit of a stretch? There's no evidence this was anything but personal and specific to the victim."

"Perhaps," I said. "But it still concerns me."

I half expected Sam to simply dismiss my fears, much like Mr. Georgianna had. But he was full of surprises, it seemed... He just sat there, thinking.

I wasn't quite sure how to address it once again, wondering if he'd even heard me in the first place.

"While I believe your fears are likely unnecessary, I will say that I can perfectly understand your reasoning behind them. These are frightening times we live in. Not only because of the happenings in Brookminster either, but the goings on in the greater world. I understand in my own way how difficult it is to go through what you have recently..." Sam stared intently at the basket of bread. "I...lost a brother in the war. About a year ago now, though it still feels like it just happened yesterday."

He lifted his gaze, which settled on me, sharp and intent.

"I know how terribly tragic it all is."

I was surprised by his transparency. "I'm very sorry to hear that," I said.

He nodded. "Yes, well, perhaps we have even more in common than we had originally thought."

"Perhaps we do," I said.

I wasn't quite sure what to make of this newfound shift in our relationship. I was used to his anger, his scolding, his scrutiny. Yet, here sitting in front of me, was a very different sort of man, one with more depth than I had originally seen.

"Now, I was serious before when I said that I would be happy to have some help," Sam said, his gravelly tone returning. "However...just like I always do, I still think there is something to be said about you keeping your distance. At least a little. For your own safety."

I looked at him, noticing the sincerity in his gaze this time. It wasn't just demanding, anger about me stepping into his territory. This time it was concern, fear for my wellbeing.

I could tell that he really wanted me to be careful.

"I do think that it is wise to keep distance between myself and these cases, of course," I said. "Especially with this one, as I have no direct connection to it."

Sam's face hardened when I did not outright agree to his request, but he said nothing.

"There is one thing I've been wondering, though," I said, hoping to change the subject. "What about the girl? The victim's daughter? What is going to happen to her?"

Sam rubbed his cheek with his palm. "Right now, she is staying with a member of the police force and his family; they have some young kids, too, and we felt it was the best place to keep her safe until we are able to find her a more permanent home."

"She doesn't have any family?" I asked.

"She does, but many of them live halfway across the country and have never met the poor girl," Sam said. "We are in discussion with some of them, but the officer's family seems eager to adopt her if no one in her family claims her."

"That's sad," I said. "She is family."

"That's what I've thought," he said. "Though it seems their family comes from some money, and her mother married someone outside of wealth, and they shunned her for it."

"How cruel," I said.

He nodded. "I'm going to see her first thing tomorrow

morning. Hopefully we will have more information by
then."

A sudden thought struck me. "Would it be all right if I
came with you?" I asked.

He regarded me for a moment. "You want to come
along?"

"Well, yes," I said. "You said you wanted my help, right?
As a civilian, maybe it would be easier for me to speak with
the girl."

It was clear he was reluctant about the idea, and was
looking for an excuse to refuse me.

After a few moments, though, he sighed. Clearly he
couldn't think of anything against it.

"Very well," he said. "You can come along. Perhaps your
presence will be of some comfort to the poor girl. I am not
known for being the most approachable of people."

"I can believe that," I said with a small smirk.

He returned it, though somewhat sheepishly.

5

The next morning, I left a sign on my door saying that I was going to remain closed for the majority of the morning, but that I would likely be back before it was time to close up for the day. I was well aware of the few customers who would likely give me an earful the next day about their needs and my lack of understanding, given their dire situations, but I tried my best to brush those worries aside. Everyone would just have to wait for their buttons and be all right with it.

I met Sam Graves at the police station, though he'd asked me to stay outside the building. "I don't want any of the boys to know about your involvement in this. Some might not take too kindly to it...especially the chief," he'd said.

That I understood rather well, knowing that if they knew he had brought me in on the case, even just to meet with Evangeline, he might be breeching some sort of rule that would otherwise forbid him from doing just that.

He stepped out of the station just ten minutes past seven, and nodded toward his car alongside the building.

"Good morning," he said to me over the roof of the car.

"Good morning to you," I said.

He unlocked the doors and we both slipped inside.

"Are you certain this is all right?" I asked as he started the car.

"Well, I already made up my mind about it," Sam said, his eyes glued to the road over his shoulder as he backed up. "No sense in going back on my word."

So no, he is already regretting it...

"So what are we going to be talking to Evangeline about?" I asked. "Just checking in on her?"

"Unfortunately, not," Sam said. "We have reason to believe that there may have been some tension between Mrs. Lowell and her landlady, Mrs. Douglas."

My eyes widened. "I heard the same rumor yesterday. Something about a fight between the two women?"

"Precisely," Sam said. "And until we have grounds to question Mrs. Douglas, our hands are tied. I hate to bring up difficult memories for the poor girl, but if we want to find out what happened to her mother..."

The officer's house was just down the street from my own, which gave me a small sense of comfort. That might prove useful if there ever was another emergency...though I hated the thought of bothering him at home when he was off duty.

"Now, for story's sake, you're working as one of our understudy stenographers, all right?" Sam asked. "We'll say it's what you did in London before you moved here to Brookminster."

"All right," I agreed.

We walked up to the entrance and Sam rapped the bronze knocker against the door.

A woman with a pale, thin face opened the door a short time later, her vibrantly red hair pulled back in a long plait behind her head. "Oh, Inspector Graves. How do you do?"

"Just fine, Mrs. Vernon," he said, inclining his head to her. "Did Phillip let you know we were coming over?"

"He did, yes," Mrs. Vernon said, pulling the door open ever so slightly more. "Won't you both come inside?"

We stepped through into the foyer, which was brightly lit and filled with family photographs on the walls. Through an archway to the right, the sounds of happy children playing could be heard.

"I'll just go get Phillip," Mrs. Vernon said. "He's back in the kitchen."

She hurried down the hall to a frosted glass door at the end, calling out to her husband as she went.

Her husband soon appeared, wearing his police uniform, though the top button of his shirt was undone. He had a kind face with sandy blonde hair that could do with a good trim, and a slightly long, bulbous nose.

"Inspector, good to see you," he said as he walked toward us, holding out his hand for Sam to shake. His gaze shifted to me. "And I must admit that I'm surprised to see you. Aren't you the one who took over the haberdashery some months ago?"

"Yes, she is, but she is also doing some work for us," Sam said before I could answer. "She used to be a stenographer in London, so she's offered to do some work for us now that she's here."

"How kind of her," Phillip said with a smile. "So you brought her here for...what? Training?"

"To see what she's capable of," Sam said. "I thought interviewing the Lowell girl might be a good place to start."

"Very well," Phillip said. "The children are through the door in here."

He led us through the doorway into the sitting room, which was cozy, furnished with all the things a family of their size might need; a chair beside the fire, a shelf full of books, and a toy chest beneath the window where three children were all huddled, scrambling for toys.

"Evangeline, someone is here to see you," said Phillip.

The girl in the middle, the oldest of the three, slowly looked up at Phillip over her shoulder. She had lovely corn-flower blonde hair, pin straight, that stretched nearly all the way down her back like a waterfall. Her eyes were crystal clear blue, bright and round. She looked at me first, and then her gaze shifted over to Sam, where her eyes widened.

"This is Inspector Sam Graves," Phillip said, kneeling down beside her. "I work with him at the police station."

"And who is she?" Evangeline asked, pointing at me.

"She is working with the police too, but she owns a little shop just down the road. You know the one that sells buttons and ribbons?"

Her face lit up with recognition.

"My name is Helen Lightholder," I said, pointing to myself. "It's nice to meet you, Evangeline.

She nodded nervously up at me.

"Evangeline, would it be all right if you were to come with Inspector Graves, Mrs. Lightholder, and I into the dining room? Just for a few minutes? I promise we won't take you away from the others for very long."

Evangeline nodded again, her eyes still glued on me as she stood up and moved away from the toy chest.

The dining room was through the kitchen and in the next room, where a worn table with many scratches told stories of fun and many meals enjoyed together as a family.

Mrs. Vernon appeared with some freshly squeezed juice in a pitcher, which she set down on the table. "Evangeline, sweetie, would you like a biscuit?"

"Before breakfast?" Evangeline asked, her eyes widening.

"Just as a special treat," Mrs. Vernon said.

Evangeline nodded, her eyes bright once again.

Phillip gestured for Sam and me to take seats beside him.

"So, Evangeline..." Sam said, putting on a smile that seemed a bit too forced. He leaned on the table, the wood creaking beneath his arms. "How are you doing today? Are you feeling well?"

The girl looked nervously back and forth between him and Phillip.

"It's all right, sweetie," Phillip said reassuringly. "Sam is a good friend. He just wants to help."

Evangeline nodded. "I'm – I'm fine," she said.

"That's good," Sam said. "Now, I came here today because I just wanted to ask you a couple of questions, all right? Easy questions that you can answer in no time."

"O – okay," Evangeline said, some of the color draining from her face.

How many times had this poor girl been interrogated since her mother's death? Too many; her reaction alone was proof of it.

"I was wondering what you might be able to tell us about Mrs. Douglas," Sam said.

I pulled the little pad of paper that Sam had pressed into

my hands outside out onto my lap, my hand poised over the page, waiting.

"Mrs. Douglas?" she asked. "Oh. She – she is the lady that let Mother and I live in her house after Father died."

My heart sank as I heard her talk about her parents, both now deceased, in such a flat tone. No...not flat. Numb. It seemed it still hadn't sunken in yet.

I scrawled the note down about the look in her eyes.

"Indeed," Sam said. "What is she like? Did she and your mother get along?"

Evangeline shook her head. "No, sir. Mrs. Douglas didn't seem to like Mother and me."

"Oh? And what makes you think that?" Sam asked.

"She would tell us how much of an inconvenience we were. I remember one day last autumn when she came in and shut the water off on us without telling us. She said she needed to fix something," Evangeline said, her shoulders curling in on herself.

Sam glanced sidelong at Phillip and me, but only briefly.

"Perhaps she'd simply forgotten," Sam said.

Evangeline shook her head. "It wasn't the only time. She also made us leave the house for a few days this past January when she wanted something worked on. She said she was going to have the part of the roof that was caving in fixed, but when we came back almost a week later, nothing had changed."

I quickly wrote that down.

"What was she doing, then?" Sam asked.

Evangeline shrugged her tiny shoulders. "I don't know. Mother thought it was because she was mad that her rent money was late. She thought she was doing it out of spite."

*That certainly wouldn't surprise me...*I thought sourly. *The house was in terrible shape just by looking at it yesterday.*

"I heard that they had a row a few weeks ago," Sam said, his brow furrowing, his tone hesitant. "Would you care to tell us about that?"

Evangeline shook her head. "N – no."

"That's all right," Sam said. "Not a problem. How about any other people that your mother knew? Were there any other people that she seemed to be upset with?"

Evangeline frowned, her fingers knotted tightly together in her lap. "Well...I don't know," she said, and I saw the first telltale signs that she was about to burst into tears.

Sam opened his mouth to speak, but I held out a hand to stop him.

Glancing over, he gave me a questioning look.

I furrowed my brow, looking back and forth between him and the poor girl. *She's going to clam up if you push too much more,* I thought.

Sam's eyes narrowed, but he sat back and gave me a permissive wave to continue on for him.

"Um...Evangeline?" I asked, smiling at her. "Hi. We just want you to know that we understand this is all very hard for you to talk about. We know you have been asked a lot of questions over the past few days, and that you are feeling very tired because of it. And more than all of that, we know how much you miss your mother, and how confusing this all is."

Evangeline's bottom lip trembled as she stared at me, nodding.

I could feel Sam's gaze on me, feel his annoyance that I might ruin this whole conversation.

"These questions are important, Evangeline, to make

sure we can help you, and find out the truth about what happened to your mother, so that something like this doesn't ever have to happen again," I said. "I know these questions might hurt a little, but if you answer them, we can help you even better. All right?"

Evangeline nodded, wiping the tears that had fallen onto her cheeks with the back of her hand. "All right," she said in a slightly shaky voice.

"Now...was there anyone else that you can think of that your mother was not happy with?" I asked. "Someone she had maybe fought with like with Mrs. Douglas?"

Evangeline's eyes widened, and I knew she'd thought of someone.

"Who was it, Evangeline?" I asked. "Who?"

The young girl, who really must have been closer to seven or eight, steeled herself, taking a deep breath and meeting my gaze with eyes that had seen far too much pain for someone her age. "I...well, I don't know his real name. My mother asked me to call him Mr. Smith when he would come to visit, but I knew that wasn't his real name. He always brought me candy when he came over for a visit, but he and Mother always used to go into the other room and talk in whispers..."

I glanced over at Sam, our eyes widening.

A love interest? I thought.

Sam's gaze hardened. "So this Mr. Smith...he and your mother were close friends?" he asked.

Evangeline nodded. "I think so. He came over a lot, especially in the mornings. I only saw him a few times, though. He was nice, but he and Mother did fight sometimes...something about Mother still loving my father..."

"Evangeline, would you be willing to describe what Mr. Smith looked like for us?" Sam asked.

Evangeline looked at me, almost as if for permission.

I nodded encouragingly.

"All right," Evangeline said. "I'll tell you."

6

I went back to my shop before nine o'clock that morning, and was able to have it open before anyone seemed to notice. Only Mrs. Waverly, who was always determined to get her shopping done as early as humanly possible, wandered by around lunchtime to tell me how disappointed she was that she couldn't pick up her order when it was convenient for her.

I closed by three, happy to have had the chance to get in almost a full day of the shop being open, and then hurried upstairs to start preparing dinner for that evening.

At half past six, my guests arrived, timely as always.

Irene and Nathanial arrived with their son Michael in tow. Nathanial was holding a box of tools when I answered the door, and Irene had a scrumptious pie that smelled as if it had been freshly pulled from the oven.

"Hello, come in, come in," I said, standing aside to let them both in.

"How are you today, dear," Irene asked as we started

toward the stairs at the back of the shop. "Are you feeling well?"

"Yes, I am, thank you," I said. "You know, I cannot thank you enough, Nathanial, for coming over to help Sidney with the stones in the fireplace. I've really started to worry about them, wondering if the whole fireplace was going to need replacing."

"It's not a problem," Nathanial said. "We've had troubles with our own fireplace in the past. It's just something that comes with these old houses. They need taking care of once in a while."

We reached the top of the stairs, and found Sidney standing over his own tool box, which was sitting on the floor beside the fireplace.

"Good evening," he said, looking over his shoulder, waving at the Driscolls.

"Hello there," Irene said.

Sidney's eyes widened. "Is that pie?"

Irene grinned. "Indeed it is. Blueberry. Freshly picked from our garden."

"Well, then I will have certainly earned my work for tonight then," Sidney said with a grin, sliding a hammer through the toolbelt that he wore.

Nathanial went over to start collaborating with Sidney, while Irene and I walked over to the kitchen where a pot was boiling merrily on the stove, and the egg timer on the counter was ticking away the time until my casserole was finished.

"Thank you for allowing me to borrow him for the evening," I said. "I know family time is important to you."

Irene smiled warmly, hugging me. "Oh, sweetheart... you're family, too. Haven't you realized that by now?"

I flushed, but I hugged her back tightly.

"Miss Helen, I picked these for you," came the voice of Michael from somewhere near my elbow.

I turned to see a bouquet of partially wilted wildflowers in his hands, two of the petals already having fallen onto the floor at his feet.

"Oh, those are beautiful Michael, thank you," I said. "I'll put them in a vase right away."

My heart was full as I walked the flowers over to the sink, and found a small bud vase inside one of the cabinets above my head.

The men had already gotten to work on the fireplace, examining the rocks that were coming loose. I'd cleared off the mantlepiece just in case they needed to remove it, and found Irene looking at the picture of Roger and I that I'd relocated to the credenza beneath the window for the time being.

"Helen, is this Roger?" she asked, turning around with her grey eyes wide, pointing at the photograph.

I was surprised at the sadness I felt when I saw her gazing upon it. It was a strange feeling, my past and my present momentarily blending together, something that I never had considered, or ever thought could happen.

"Yes, it is," I said, putting the spoon for the boiling potatoes down on the ceramic rest and wiping my hands off on the apron I wore.

"Why haven't I seen this before?" Irene asked, picking up the photo and examining it, looking back and forth between it and me.

"I've had most of his things put away," I said, walking over to the sitting room to stand beside her. "It was too hard to look at."

"So what made you want to bring it out now?" she asked.

"Well..." I said. "I keep having these dreams about him at night, and...I don't know. I guess I realized that I needed to stop trying to run from my past and just give myself the time to heal. Hiding from it was not helping me, and I needed to admit that to myself."

"That's very brave of you," Irene said. She turned back to the photo, smiling.

"Where was this picture taken?" she asked.

"During our honeymoon in Italy," I said. "About two years ago, in fact."

"Well, I think it's very nice to have some reminder of him around your home," Irene said. "He was an important part of your life, after all."

"I agree," I said. "I also pulled some of his letters out and tucked them into a shadowbox that is hanging in my room. I like to take them out at night and read them."

"Oh, Helen, that's so sweet," Irene said, a sad smile appearing on her pretty face.

"This is your husband?"

We turned and saw Nathanial and Sidney standing behind us, peering over our shoulders at the photograph.

"Yes," I said, flushing slightly. I hadn't anticipated so much attention to be given to this picture.

"He's quite handsome, isn't he?" Irene asked.

"He was," I agreed.

"And I'm sure he was a good man, too," Nathaniel offered kindly, before he and Sidney turned back to their work on the fireplace.

"So how often did you see Roger when you were together?" Irene asked, setting the photograph down, shifting it ever so slightly so the light didn't glint off the glass. "From what you've said, it wasn't all that frequently."

I started back toward the kitchen. "It wasn't nearly as often as I would have liked," I said. "The war began just after we were married, and he had to spend most of him time in London."

"What sort of work did your husband do?" Sidney asked, glancing over his shoulder as Nathanial knelt down beside his tool chest and started to search for something.

I glanced over at them, my face flooding with color. "I... well, to be honest, I never really knew much about it," I said. "It involved the military or the government or something. He couldn't talk about it much. He was able to come home for three days out of the month, but those three days never felt long enough. He wasn't even able to come home for Christmas..."

"So I take it that you were not together when he was killed?" Sidney asked. "You weren't in London?"

Silence fell over the room, the sort of silence that sat heavily on us all.

"No," I said. "No, I was at my parents' home in Plymouth."

"Well...I'm sorry," Sidney said.

It was incredibly uncomfortable after that. I busied myself with finishing the potatoes, and Irene stood help-lessly in the sitting room.

Nathanial cleared his throat behind me. "I heard today that the police have been contacting Evangeline Lowell's family, trying to find someone who will take her in. Unfortu-nately, it seems that no one wants her."

I was drawn back into the present, recalling the morning I'd had with Sam Graves.

"That poor dear," Irene said. "Nathanial, maybe we can take her in if they can't find anywhere else for her to go."

"That might not be a bad idea," I said, looking at her over my shoulder, not wanting to hide behind my own frustrations any longer. "Her family apparently disowned them when her mother married her father."

All three heads swiveled around to stare at me.

"How do you know that?" Irene asked.

I hesitated. "Well...Sam Graves told me, actually."

"Sam Graves?" Irene asked. "What was he doing telling you anything about that case?"

I turned the stove off and hoisted the pot off the burner, carting it over to the sink where the colander waited for me. "He...asked for my help," I said, not looking over at her when I spoke.

"Why?" she asked. "He has been adamant about you staying out of all this."

"I know," I said. "But he told me that he sees value in my help, considering how involved I was with discovering the truth about my aunt's death. He seemed eager, even, to allow me to get information in ways that he as an inspector never could."

Irene's face hardened, and she folded her arms over her chest. "I have a hard time believing that he would be so willing to have you involved, especially after he was so frustrated with you about the Polish beggar."

"Yes, well..." I said. "He seemed willing enough to have me along this morning."

Irene rolled her eyes, huffing in disbelief.

Sidney said, "What did he need help with this morning?"

I nervously met his gaze for but a moment before

turning away. "Well...I went with him to speak to Mrs. Lowell's little girl, Evangeline."

"You *what?*" Irene asked. She looked over at her husband. "Nathanial, can he really be doing this? She isn't a part of the police force. How can he – "

"Inspector Graves can do what he pleases, unfortunately," Nathanial said, wiping his hands on an old cloth he'd brought with him. "Though I am surprised that he would ask a civilian for help. Why did he want you to go with him?"

"For one, I was able to get information from the girl that he could not, being as curt as he always is," I said, somewhat indignant. "We came by the knowledge that her mother had been in a fight with her landlady, Mrs. Douglas, and – "

"I've done some work for her," Irene said, her face paling. "She's a right bitter woman, let me tell you."

"She certainly is," Nathanial said, his brow furrowing. "Do the police suspect she was the one who killed Mrs. Lowell?"

"Well, just between us, she's one of the suspects," I said. "Though I'm not certain that she is the primary one, especially given what we learned this morning about the mother's secret lover."

"Lover?" all three asked at the same time.

I stared around at them all, my voice catching in my throat. *Perhaps I shouldn't have mentioned that...*

"Who was it?" Irene asked.

"Well, the girl wasn't entirely sure," I said. "Her mother asked Evangeline to call the man Mr. Smith when he would come over, but she was almost certain that wasn't his real name. Sam asked her if she would be willing to give a description of the man so that the police might be able to find him, as they'd had no idea of his existence..."

"Everyone always seems to have sordid pasts, don't they?" Sidney asked, shaking his head as he turned back around to the wall with a tub of some sort of concrete in his hand.

"That's a rather hard view of people," Irene said. "I never took you for a cynic, Mr. Mason."

Sidney gave her a wry smile before scooping some of the mixture up with a trowel, and beginning to slather it on the cracks in the fireplace between the large stones.

"What did she say he looked like?" Nathanial asked, also picking up a trowel to help Sidney. "I can't imagine a girl as young as she would be able to give an accurate description."

"Oh, it was quite descriptive, actually," I said. "She told us that the man was about as tall as Sam was, and that he was very thin. She said that he wore glasses, and that he had a scar on the back of his right hand."

"Did he have dark hair?" Nathanial asked.

I looked over at him. "Yes, he did."

"Nathanial, do you know who this man is?" Irene asked.

"I might," Nathanial said, his brow furrowing. "But I certainly would regret it if it's who I think it is."

7

"Why would you say that?" Irene asked, walking over to her husband, a look of concern etched on her face.

Nathanial lowered his arm; he'd been scraping more of the concrete in between the rocks that were beginning to come loose on my fireplace.

Sidney stopped as well, regarding Nathanial with as much curiosity as Irene and I were.

"Well..." Nathanial said. "I realize there might be quite a few men in this world today who have scars on the back of their hands, and who wear glasses...but if it's someone who lives here in Brookminster, then this was the sort of man that Mrs. Lowell never should have been involved with in the first place."

"Why's that?" Sidney asked. "Is he a dangerous sort of man?"

"In a sense," Nathanial said.

"Oh, stop playing games," Irene said, giving her husband

a rather sour look. "Who is it? And what's the matter with him?"

"His name is William Fenton," Nathanial said. "And many of us believe he is cursed."

"Cursed?" Irene and I asked together.

"Oh, come now, Nathanial. Surely you cannot be serious," his wife said.

"Oh, but I am," Nathanial said. "He works at the bookshop down by the watermill, and I have never met a man who is more prone to accident than he."

"That doesn't make him dangerous," Irene said.

"Doesn't it?" he said. "He managed to start a fire in his house when he sneezed while holding a candle, nearly burned the whole place down. And he somehow managed to get himself caught underneath an avalanche of books at his own shop, which very nearly killed him. He was in the hospital for two weeks with broken ribs and a sprained wrist."

"So he's a clumsy sort," Sidney said, returning his trowel to the fireplace. "I don't think that makes him dangerous."

"You haven't heard how he managed to get that cut on the back of his hand…" Nathanial said.

"How do you know this man so well?" Irene asked. "What did you say his name was? Fenton?"

"Exactly," Nathanial said. "And he picks up the orders for his books at the same delivery house where I pick up our tea at the edge of town."

"At Roddrick's?" Sidney asked.

"That's the one," Nathanial said. "Still, I'm surprised that anyone would have been romantically involved with him, given that he's about as jumpy as a mouse."

"Does he not deserve happiness?" Irene asked.

"I never said that," Nathanial said. "Just that I'm amazed that he was able to approach a woman. He can barely speak with his customers."

"I still don't understand why you would think a woman shouldn't be with someone like him," Irene said, clearly upset with her husband's words. "That's just preposterous."

"I was only thinking of the woman's safety, my dear," Nathanial said.

I frowned. "You don't think that one of his notorious accidents is what caused Mrs. Lowell's death, do you?"

"I wouldn't rule it out," Nathanial said.

"Oh, Nathanial, that's ridiculous," Irene said. "Why on earth wouldn't he have come forward with it, then? Even if it was an accident?"

"I don't know," Nathanial said. "Maybe he didn't know how to confess."

These thoughts troubled me all through dinner, but I didn't voice my opinion on the matter. Nathanial and Sidney finished the patching of the fireplace, assuring me that it was as good as new now and would hold out. Irene hugged me tightly before leaving, in a very motherly sort of way, and even though she didn't say it, I knew she wanted me to stay safe. She clearly disagreed with Sam Graves' decision to let me help with the case, but I understood that she meant well.

I began to wonder if Sam knew about this William Fenton fellow. I also wondered why on earth Mrs. Lowell wouldn't have asked Evangeline to call him by his real name. Was it so that he would remain discreet? And when Evangeline said they fought, she said it was about her mother's feelings for her father. Was she feeling guilty about seeing another man so soon after his death? Perhaps she wanted to avoid gossip and speculation?

All these questions chased themselves around in my head as I lay down to sleep that night, and filled my dreams as I walked along a dark hall with Evangeline's hand in my own, asking her to point out all the people her mother knew. It was too many to count, and there were too many possibilities.

When I awoke the next morning, I was quite flustered, and determined to check out this man for myself before bringing any information to Sam Graves...along with an apology. He would have wanted me to bring this information to him immediately, I knew, but I would have to explain that I told Nathanial, Irene, and Sidney about what Evangeline had said the night before, and the more I thought about it, the more I realized that I probably shouldn't have done that in the first place.

He was not going to be pleased.

So, to make up for my actions, I would go and investigate this information, so that I could then tell him that my sources were my own and that he just had to trust me, thus protecting Nathanial and Irene from Sam's scrutiny.

The hours ticked by in the haberdashery that day. I found myself glancing up at the clock far too often, only to find that the minute hand had barely moved. Business was slow, as well, tempting me to close up early so I could wander down to the bookshop and meet this William Fenton for myself.

I resisted the urge, however, and made it to the afternoon. After closing up, I quickly changed and headed out before half past three, eager to reach the shop before he closed it.

The bookshop was on the same road as Mrs. Lowell's rental cottage was, just further along. I was amazed that I'd never seen it, though it wasn't often that I made it this far to the other side of the village. It was a charming establishment, with large front windows of leaded glass, and books stacked high on shelves that could be seen inside. The door was also mostly windowed, with a hand-carved sign on the front declaring; *Fenton's Fabulous Fictions (And Non)*.

I pulled open the door, and walked inside.

A bell sounded somewhere near the back of the shop, which was entirely obstructed from my view as the shelves were so high and densely packed. The precariousness of the shop itself very nearly convinced me that what Nathanial said about Mr. Fenton being accident prone was true.

I saw painted, wooden signs hanging alongside the shelves, directing me toward history, poetry, and biographies. As I turned around the corner of a shelf, I found more pointing to fiction, adventure, and children's.

There were other people in the labyrinth of the store, hidden away behind shelves, their noses buried in all manner of books. There was soft music playing from some unknown source; Mozart, I was very nearly certain.

"Ah, good afternoon."

I almost jumped out of my skin at the sound of another person's voice. I wheeled around and found myself staring at a thin, dark haired man with round spectacles. He wrung his hands together in front of himself, but there was a kind smile on his face.

"I thought I heard someone come in," he said, pushing his glasses up the bridge of his nose. I noticed a pinkish, silver scar across the back of his hand that stretched from the joint at his thumb all the way to the knuckle below his little finger.

And it was on his right hand.

"Uh, yes," I said.

"First time customer?" he asked.

"Yes, yes I am," I said.

"Very good," he said. "Well, my name is William Fenton. If you need any help finding anything, I – I would be happy to locate it for you. I have a little bit of everything here. E – even some first editions at the back."

"How wonderful," I said.

He nodded, looking down at his shoes, wringing his hands once more. "W – well, I'll be off, then. Just let me know if you need any help."

"I certainly will," I said. "Thank you very much, Mr. Fenton."

He nodded, bowed ever so slightly, and turned, hurrying away back through the maze of shelves and stacks of books.

*He was certainly nervous...*I thought. *Just like Nathanial said.*

He was kind, though, and even in his unease, there was some charm there, something rather endearing. If he would smile, I would have thought him to be rather good looking.

I slowly started down the same path that Mr. Fenton had, careful to keep my footsteps light so as to not disturb the other shoppers, but also to not alert Mr. Fenton to my approach.

As I rounded another row of shelves, the end of the back counter came into view, and I glimpsed the edge of Mr. Fenton's elbow as he organized a stack of books.

I ducked behind the next shelf, moving quietly parallel to where he stood. Between a few of the cookbooks that were arranged by cuisine, I could just see him standing behind the counter, books stacked precariously behind him, likely waiting to be sorted. They stretched far over his head, well out of my line of sight.

If he bumped those they would likely fall right upon his head.

I plucked a Yorkshire cookbook from the shelf and flipped it open in my arms, pretending to scan the recipe there for a redcurrant cobbler.

Through the shelf, I could see him opening the front cover of the book, reading something, and then scrawling a note down on the pad beside him. He then closed the book and moved it to his other side, atop another stack of books that was quickly becoming too tall.

As he flipped open another book, he winced, pulling his finger away from the page. Examining it closely, he squinted, his nose wrinkling, before shoving the finger into his mouth.

Paper cut, I thought. *He truly is accident prone.*

I watched him for some time, the cookbook still propped open in my hands, noting just how often he managed to harm himself. At one point, he dropped a book on his foot. And at another, when he was trying to set his pen down, it went flying instead and hit him square between the eyes.

It was almost amusing, except I felt sorry for the fellow.

A quarter of an hour later, an older woman with golden hair that was fading to white approached the counter, two thin books in her hands. "Good afternoon, William."

"Well, hello there, Mrs. Charles. How are you this fine day?" he asked, holding out his hand for her books.

"I'm quite well, dear, thank you," the woman said. "And...how are you doing?"

There was weight to her question; Mr. Fenton had noticed it, too.

He licked his lips, setting the books down on the counter as gently as if they were living. "I...well, I'm doing well enough, I suppose."

The woman made a pitiful, sad sound, and stepped closer. "Are you really?" she asked. "I can imagine that with all that has happened, you would need some time to heal... yet here you are, back at work."

"Well, it's certainly better than sitting home all alone," he said. "It helps keep my mind occupied."

"That's good to hear," Mrs. Charles said.

Do they mean Mrs. Lowell? I thought. *If they do, then this truly is Evangeline's Mr. Smith.*

Mrs. Charles reached across the counter and laid her hand on William's. "I know that you miss Abigail," she said in a murmur. "We all do. She was such a sweet young girl, and what happened to her was utterly tragic. It wasn't fair that you two had your happiness ripped from you so soon."

William bowed his head, only nodding in response.

"Have you heard what is happening to Evangeline?" Mrs. Charles asked. "I spoke with Lucille, who is friends with the officer's sister who has taken her in for the time being..."

"I did, yes," he said. "I wish there was something I could do to help, but...it really isn't my place. Not anymore."

"But it should have been," Mrs. Charles said firmly, squeezing his hand. "You were planning to marry her, William. You had the ring, didn't you? And it was robbed from you, just like that – "

"Mrs. Charles..." William said, laying his free hand over hers, stopping her. "I understand your concern. And I appreciate it. I truly do. But she's gone, and there is unfortunately nothing that I can do about it."

Mrs. Charles' face fell, but she gave him a tight smile. "You're right…" she said. "I'm very sorry, my dear."

"As am I," he said. "As am I."

From there, she paid for her books, and he packed them up in some thick brown paper, but not without cutting himself on the edge of it once again. Freshly bandaged, he passed her the books.

"You take care, William," she said. "And if you need anything, come and see Patrick and me, won't you?"

"Of course, Mrs. Charles," he said.

He waved at her as she started toward the door, but as soon as her back was turned, his face fell, and it was as if he had aged twenty years.

My heart stirred. It was clear that he loved Mrs. Lowell, as strange as Evangeline's testimony about him had been.

*He wanted to marry her…*I thought. *I wonder if that's what he and Mrs. Lowell had been fighting about before she died…*

The bell signaling the front door chimed above Mr. Fenton's head, and he glanced up at it, as if the sound alone had brought him back to reality.

He set the stack of books he'd been sorting aside, and started out from around the counter…when a woman in a bright pink coat appeared around the corner.

"Mr. Fenton! I was hoping I would find you here."

8

I spun around, burying my nose back in the cookbook, the recipe not having changed even once since I opened the book, as another customer strolled past me.

I pretended to be engrossed with the measurements of the currants, mouthing the ingredients as I read the instructions.

The customer continued on past, and as soon as she had disappeared around the corner, I turned on my heel and peered between the shelves.

My eyes widened as I saw the dark-haired woman leaning on the counter, familiarly close with Mr. Fenton... who looked all too uncomfortable about the situation in which he found himself.

"Oh, William, it's been far too long since I've seen you," said the woman in a rather whiny, high pitched voice. She cooed to him as if he were an infant.

"Y – yes, I suppose," Mr. Fenton said, taking a deliberate

step backward. He bumped into the teetering books behind him, which wobbled threateningly.

He threw his weight against it.

My shoulders tensed.

The tower stopped sliding toward him, and his shoulders sagged as he stepped back away.

When he turned, the woman was still there, practically lying across the counter.

I could just make out her profile. She was a rather feline looking woman, with a small, button nose, a curling smile, and pouting lips.

"I've missed you," she said in what reminded me of a purr.

"H – Have you?" Mr. Fenton said, pulling a handkerchief out from his front shirt pocket. He dabbed at his glistening forehead. "Is there, um...Is there something I can help you with, Miss Harmon?"

Miss Harmon chuckled, resting her hand on her chin as she grinned up at Mr. Fenton. "I'm much better now that I can see you, of course."

Mr. Fenton did his best to avoid looking at her. He busied himself with the list he'd been making before Mrs. Charles had walked in. "Well, if you decide you need my help, then please don't – don't hesitate to ask me – "

"I am asking, you foolish man," she teased, laying a finger against his chest. She twirled absentminded shapes across the buttons of his shirt. "I was hoping that you could help me with my loneliness..."

He slowly pushed her hand away. "I've already told you...I have a great deal on my mind, and after losing Abigail, I – "

The woman's demeanor changed instantaneously. She stood up straight, withdrawing her hand, and sneered at poor Mr. Fenton. "Abigail, Abigail, *Abigail*. Is there nothing else to discuss these days?"

I blinked. I couldn't believe what I'd just heard.

His eyes narrowed as he looked at her, and his face fell sheepishly.

She made a noise of disgust, rolling her eyes rather dramatically. "All I ever hear about anymore is *Abigail*. Or that daughter of hers. What was her name? Amanda or something?"

"Evangeline," he said, a great deal more curtly than he had before. "Listen, Tessa...I have a great deal of work to do today, so...if you'll excuse me..."

He deftly moved around her, averting his eyes, and headed off into the bookshelves.

Miss Harmon stared after him, her eyes narrow slits, chewing on her tongue. Her sour expression disappeared just a moment later, though, and a sneaky smile spread up the side of her face. Her hips swayed as she threw her purse over her shoulder, and strutted away from the counter in the opposite direction from the one Mr. Fenton had gone.

With nothing more than a hunch, I slid the cookbook back on the shelf, and decided that Miss Harmon might be the better person to follow. Her utter disdain for Mrs. Lowell's death was such a surprise.

I headed out of the bookshop just after Miss Harmon had disappeared through the exit, her pink coat fluttering in the wind caught by the door.

She started down the street, her hips swaying as if she had someone to impress.

I followed at a relatively safe distance, keeping her in sight, but ensuring that she would not be suspicious if she were to turn around and see me. I was certain she hadn't seen me in the bookshop, so she wouldn't even recognize me.

It was clear that something was going on between her and William Fenton. At least, it certainly was one way.

She took a sharp turn, and I hurried to catch up with her. Was she heading home?

Or perhaps she was heading to Mr. Fenton's house?

I was surprised when she turned down Ivy Street, and soon after, headed toward the teahouse.

My heart skipped. This was both a wonderful opportunity, as well as a frightening happenstance.

I hurried inside, my eyes scanning the room.

Miss Harmon's bright pink was distinct among the other patrons, as she walked up to Irene, who was standing at one of the tables, clearing away the dirty teacups and crumbed plates.

"I would like a table near the window," Miss Harmon said.

Irene looked at her, her eyes widening. "You're welcome to one," Irene said. "You may sit wherever there is a free table."

Miss Harmon tossed her black hair over her shoulder, and strutted over to a table in front of the window.

I made eye contact with Irene, and nodded toward the kitchen.

She started toward it at the same time I did, and we met together just inside the swinging door.

"What's the matter?" Irene asked. "You look troubled."

"That woman who just came in? In the pink coat?" I asked.

"Tessa Harmon, yes," Irene said. "What's the matter? What happened?"

My gaze darted back toward Tessa, who brushed her dark hair from her eyes, her smirk set firmly in place.

"Come with me," I said, grabbing Irene by the elbow and ushering her toward the kitchen.

I was grateful that she didn't pester me too much before we were safely hidden behind the swinging door. The air smelled of cinnamon and vanilla bean, which would have tempted me into asking her what she was making, but I resisted, my mind already scolding me about my distractions.

"I found Mrs. Lowell's sweetheart," I said in a rushed whisper.

"You what?" Irene asked, her brow furrowing. She folded her arms, and I noticed a streak of icing along her forearm. "Helen, I can't believe you're still trying to involve yourself in all this. I'm starting to think you have a death wish, or that you've simply lost your mind because of the grief you are feeling after losing Roger – "

"No, listen to me," I said, laying a hand on her arm, stopping her in mid-sentence. "I really don't think it was him. He's not the type. Owns a bookshop, really nervous, all that. But the woman who just walked in, that Tessa? I think she is in love with him."

"With Mrs. Lowell's secret lover?" Irene asked, now interested.

I nodded. "I just saw her with him. If she had it her way, she would have been over the counter and all over him."

"What did he do?" Irene asked.

"It was clear he was trying to be kind," I said. "But he wasn't at all interested, not in the least. And the strangest part was that Tessa complained about people talking about Mrs. Lowell so much, as if she was still alive and just a nuisance."

"Really?" Irene asked. She frowned, rubbing her cheek in thought. "Well, even I must admit that she is not the nicest woman in town. Very narcissistic, with nothing more than contempt for anything that doesn't have to do with her...but to fall in love with a book seller? I imagined she would have sought after some sort of businessman in London..."

"It surprised me as well," I said. "He is quite good looking, I suppose, but not the sort of man that women would typically fight over."

I turned and pushed open the door to the restaurant, locating Tessa easily in her pink.

My eyes widened when I realized there was another woman sitting at the table, someone with as much flamboyance as she seemed to have.

"Someone's with her," I said.

Irene moved to the door, and I ducked down so she could peer out over the top of my head.

"That's Madeline Woods. She's quite the piece of work, if I may say so."

"How so?" I asked.

"She's a terrible gossip," Irene said. "Very plainly nice when she speaks with you, but then will twist your words and utterly humiliate you to whomever she decides to speak with next." She shook her head, sighing. "I must admit, she is perfect company for Tessa Harmon."

The women seemed happy enough, chattering away,

their heads bent toward one another, their lips peeled back in troubling smiles, as if exchanging the darkest of secrets.

My nerves steeled. "I need to hear what they're talking about."

"What?" Irene asked. "Why?"

"What if they're talking about Mr. Fenton?" I asked. "The bookshop owner," I added, seeing the confused look on Irene's face. "What if she is somehow responsible for what happened to Mrs. Lowell?"

Irene's brow wrinkled with worry, and she bit down on the inside of her lip. "I suppose it's possible," she said.

We agreed then to take turns heading out and serving the women. I knew that Tessa wouldn't recognize me, as I was almost certain that she wouldn't have seen me in the bookshop. I decided to be extra cautious, though, by tying my hair back and borrowing some of Irene's deep red lipstick to give myself a quick change of appearance.

Wearing a freshly laundered apron and with notebook in hand, I pasted a smile on and wandered out into the dining area, Irene following close behind me.

I wandered over to the table where the women were sitting, still bending their heads together, the clear glee on their faces making my stomach twist into knots.

"Good afternoon, ladies," I said, approaching them. "How are we doing?"

The scathing look that Tessa gave me sent chills down my spine. She gave me a very clear, deliberate look up and down, the condescension clear on her face.

"We'll have some tea," Tessa said. "That is what this place serves, right?"

"Of course," I said, my false smile still in place. "Would either of you care for any tea cakes, biscuits, or sandw – "

"Did we *ask* for any of those?" asked Madeline Woods, arching an eyebrow, her deep green eyes surrounded in a smoky black eyeliner.

"No, but I was not certain that you knew what we offered here – " I said.

"Bring us the tea," Tessa snapped. "Now, would be preferable."

I flipped the notebook shut and turned, still smiling, and started back off toward the kitchens.

"Did you hear anything?" Irene asked as we passed by one another.

"No," I said. "See what you can find out."

I made my way into the kitchen and began to prepare their tea, tapping my fingers impatiently upon the counter as I waited.

Irene stepped back inside the kitchen just as I was pouring the tea from the kettle on the stove into one of the ornate pots that Irene liked to serve it with. Her eyes were wide, and her cheeks pale.

"What's the matter?" I asked.

"I managed to overhear just a little of their conversation," Irene said, reaching for a napkin rolled up and tucked in the basket beside the door, ready for a new table. She dabbed at her forehead, staring at something in the distance. "You were right about her feelings for that bookshop owner. Mr. Fenton was his name, correct?"

I nodded as I pulled two matching teacups from the shelf where Irene and Nathanial kept them all, ready for guest use. "Yes, Fenton. She admitted as much?"

She nodded as well, swallowing hard as if something was stuck in her throat. "More than that, she seems quite pleased that Mrs. Lowell is out of the way now."

"What did she say exactly?" I asked.

Irene's lips pursed, and she exhaled sharply through her nose. *"With that Abigail out of the way now, nothing is standing between Mr. Fenton and I. Isn't that wonderful? We can finally be together...if only he would see it, too."*

I frowned. "I understand being in love with someone, but to be so utterly dismissive of poor Mrs. Lowell?"

"That's what I thought, such a lack of remorse..." Irene said. "And Miss Woods did nothing but encourage her, assuring her that he would come around eventually, no man could resist such a lovely, persistent woman."

I folded my arms. "Well, that's not much of a surprise," I said. "Given what you said about her character. And if they really are friends, which they clearly seem to be, why wouldn't she encourage her friend in her love affairs?"

"I suppose," Irene said.

The door to the kitchen swung open, and Nathanial strolled in.

"Irene, I – " he said, and his eyes swept through the room, falling first upon his wife, and then the next second upon me. "Oh, hello, Helen."

"Sweetheart, what are you doing home already?" Irene asked, glancing at the clock on the wall. "You said you wouldn't be home for another three hours."

Worry creased Nathanial's face. "Yes, well...I heard some news that I thought you might want to be aware of. You as well, Helen."

The skin on my neck prickled. "What sort of news?"

He reached for a newspaper he'd tucked beneath his arm. Setting it on the counter, he spread it open wide.

A blurry photograph of what looked like a prison was on the front page, along with the title, *CASE CLOSED;*

THE MURDERS OF BROOKSMINSTER PUT TO BED AT LAST.

"You both may want to read that article," Nathanial said. "It seems some anonymous source has claimed that all the murders that have happened in the village are related."

9

"This writer claims that all of the murders in Brookminster are related somehow?" I asked, leaning over the paper with Irene, who was quickly scanning the words.

"Seems that way," Nathanial said. "Go ahead and read it."

The writer was rather long winded, giving a lengthy history of the dark deeds that apparently had occurred in Brookminster over the last one hundred years, describing the town as perfect on the surface, but dark and rotten on the inside.

The heart of the article, though, was a complete shock... and something that I would never have expected.

"I must admit, I'm confused," I said, looking up at Irene and Nathanial. "This writer thinks that Mrs. Lowell's killing, as well as the killing of all the others in town in the last few months...were because of a prison camp outside of town?"

Nathanial leaned against the counter, folding his arms.

"We all know that isn't true, but we still don't know who killed Mrs. Lowell, do we?"

"Where is this camp?" I asked. "I've never even heard of it."

"There aren't many outside of Brookminster that do know about it," Irene said, giving her husband a nervous look. "It's on a farm to the north of here, certainly far enough away from the town, and heavily guarded, no less."

"And this is where what sort of prisoners reside?" I asked, my eyes narrowing.

"Well..." Nathanial said, shifting uncomfortably. "During the war, it seems they've been keeping German prisoners of war there."

My jaw dropped open. "They're keeping Germans... here?" I asked.

"It's far enough removed from the bigger cities that they aren't a safety concern," Nathanial said. "And if they were to escape, they wouldn't get far before someone more familiar with the area would be able to catch up with them."

"But what about Brookminster?" I asked. "What about our safety?"

"Helen, dear, it is safe," Irene said. "They have all been put to work under heavy guard, farming the land. The food they dig up is sent to our troops, and they are paying for their crimes against – "

"Farming seems far too easy," I said. "These men have killed our soldiers, dropped bombs on our cities – "

"I know," Nathanial said. "I know," he said again, more gently. "But they really are under heavy guard. And none of the soldiers have ever tried to escape. I would know. I've been there, and asked around."

"Been there?" I asked. "Why?"

"His brother is one of the guards," Irene said.

"I see," I said.

"Who is this writer?" Irene asked, pointing to the newspaper lying on the counter. "They're claiming that one of the Germans *did* escape, and they were the ones responsible for Mrs. Lowell's death."

Nathanial picked up the paper, examining the article once again. "I'm not certain; it says it is anonymous. But we can easily dismiss the whole article as nonsense, since we all know very well that an escaped German soldier was not the one who killed anyone else that has died here recently."

"Can we dismiss it so readily, though?" Irene asked. "The war is escalating, and I imagine that camp is becoming full. When was the last time you saw your brother? A month ago? Perhaps two?"

Nathanial scratched his chin. "I cannot imagine things would have changed so drastically there in that short amount of time," he said.

"So you are saying it is impossible for a prisoner to escape?" I asked.

"Well, perhaps not *impossible*," Nathanial said. "But certainly very difficult, given the guards are all armed and trained as well."

I said, "What if a prisoner did manage to escape, entered the village for whatever reason, possibly to steal supplies, and had a violent encounter with Mrs. Lowell, maybe because she caught him in the act of stealing? What if he killed her and then disappeared? Meanwhile, nobody up at the prison camp has even noticed he is gone."

"That seems like a stretch, dear," Irene said, but she looked up at Nathanial. "Though, I must admit...I, too, have wondered if it has been guarded enough these last few months. Your brother and the others must be getting so utterly tired of the work they do...and I know I'm not alone in this worry. Many others in town have expressed concern about it as well."

"But none of these soldiers could possibly have been the killer," Nathanial said to his wife. "We already know who killed Helen's aunt, as well as the beggar. We know who they were, and the incidents weren't related at all."

"Can we rule anything out at this point, though?" I asked. "Some soldiers can be incredibly skilled. Many of them are trained to be spies, to withstand torture. How can we be utterly certain that one of these hasn't used their incredible training to do just like the writer said?"

Nathanial sighed. "I suppose anything is possible, isn't it?" he asked. "But in truth, we have no idea who the writer is."

"Clearly someone the publishers at the newspaper thought highly enough of to add it to the morning post," Irene said. "With a sizable article on the front page, no less."

"I'm not one to trust writers for the post, just because their article was published," Nathanial said. "Not these days."

"Well, I know one person who we could speak with to get all of this cleared up," I said. "Sam Graves would certainly know something about it."

"That he likely would," Nathanial said. "He might be the best one to bring this to. I'm certain he's seen the article. The police are all likely in an uproar today, trying to calm any concerned townsfolk who inevitably will have dropped by the station demanding answers."

Irene looked over at me, like a mother scolding a child.

"You want to go and tell him about Mr. Fenton and Miss Harmon, don't you?" she asked.

Nathanial's face became concerned, and he straightened up. "Mr. Fenton? What about him?"

"You were right about him. He is apparently the man who was attempting to woo Mrs. Lowell," Irene said.

My eyes widened. "I can't believe I forgot to tell you...he wasn't just trying to woo her, Irene. He had planned to propose. He had the ring and everything."

"Mr. Fenton was the Mr. Smith that Evangeline was talking about after all?" Nathanial asked. He shook his head. "When you described him, I could hardly believe a man like him would have ever been able to pursue someone like Mrs. Lowell."

"He seemed perfectly harmless," I said. "Perhaps a bit accident prone, just as you said, but it's quite clear he has a good, gentle heart."

"That he does," Nathanial said. "A bit of a coward, though."

"I wondered about that myself," I said. "I think he believes he waited too long to let Mrs. Lowell know how he felt."

"How tragic," Irene said. "Not only had Abigail managed to find love again after her husband died, but then before anything could ever come of it, she passed away."

"I'm saddened for poor Mr. Fenton," I said. "He is the one who has to now live with the reality of her death...and he wants nothing more than to be able to do something for Evangeline, but doesn't feel as if it is his place."

"But I don't understand why you mentioned Tessa Harmon," Nathanial said, his brow furrowing. "What does she have to do with any of this?"

Irene and I glanced at one another. I certainly wasn't one for gossip, but something was not sitting right about that woman and her attitude toward the deceased.

"She seems to be in love with Mr. Fenton as well," Irene answered for me. "Making this whole ordeal just a bit more complicated, it seems."

"Another suspect, then?" Nathanial asked.

"I suppose so," Irene said. She looked over at me. "I take it you're going to take all of this to Inspector Graves?"

"I suppose I should," I said. "He might not even know that Mr. Fenton had another admirer."

"While I can't imagine that anyone like Tessa would ever be able to do something like take someone's life, I certainly wouldn't rule out her utter dislike of poor Abigail Lowell."

"My thoughts exactly," I said.

I glanced toward the door, and back at the tea I'd poured into the teapot nearly a quarter of an hour before.

"Speaking of Miss Harmon, I suppose I should get their tea out to them," I said. "Before they decide to go and spread terrible rumors about your teahouse's lack of service."

I remade the tea and hurried it out to the ladies, who surprisingly hadn't even noticed I'd been gone.

"Just set it down and shoo," Tessa said, glowering up at me. "Can't you see we're in the middle of a conversation?"

"My apologies," I said, inclining my head. "I won't bother you any longer."

I turned away, my skin crawling.

*With any luck, I won't be the one to bother you again...*I thought as I walked away from their table. *But who knows what Sam Graves might think when I tell him how much you despised Abigail Lowell.*

10

I waited another hour before I left the teahouse. I knew it would be suspicious if I were to wait only on Tessa Harmon and her friend, so I helped Irene with some other customers, all of whom were a great deal more kind to me. I always found I enjoyed working at the teahouse, as it gave me a chance to interact with the community more easily, and without having to count buttons or spools of thread.

Tessa Harmon and her friend left soon after finishing their tea, which they complained about far too loudly, saying it was subpar quality, even for these difficult times.

Irene just glared at them as they left. "Don't they know that we still buy the very best tea available, straight from India? They likely wouldn't buy tea that expensive, even for themselves at home."

I bid her and Nathanial goodbye, and asked Nathanial if I could borrow the newspaper so that I could bring the article to Sam.

"I hope you know what you're doing," he said in an undertone, passing it to me. "You are worrying Irene something awful. She is beside herself most of the time, worrying about the situations that you are getting yourself into."

"Everything is fine," I said. "All I am doing is relaying information. I'm not chasing after the killer this time."

"As far as you know," Nathanial said. "Just...please, be careful, all right? For our sake?"

"I will," I said, and made my way from the teahouse.

I was surprised about Nathanial's comment. I had known that Irene was displeased with my involvement in all this, yet to hear it so starkly from him made it all the more real to me.

I needed to be careful. My life wasn't just about me any longer. There were people who cared for me, even here in Brookminster.

The clouds had returned in the sky, making it seem much later than early evening. I shivered as a cool gust of wind rushed down the street.

I turned into the wind, starting toward the police station.

I hadn't walked more than three houses away when a chill raced down my back.

I glanced over my shoulder, half expecting Tessa Harmon to be standing there, having somehow overheard the conversation I'd had with Irene.

No one was standing there, though.

Fear, hot and stinging, surged through my veins.

*This is just like the last time...*I thought.

I picked up my pace, wanting to put as much distance between myself and whatever it was that I felt was after me.

It was just the wind, I assured myself. *You haven't been outside properly in days. When was the last time you smelled the fresh air?*

The air held the sharp scent of rain, and smelled of coming storms, and lingering heat.

I only walked a few more steps before the feeling returned.

There was no one else on the road with me; not up ahead, and not behind. And yet, I was utterly convinced that someone was watching me.

But who? And where?

I searched around, my eyes narrowing as I squinted through the hazy, cloudy evening.

A movement out of the corner of my eye caught my attention, and I whirled around.

A shadow seemed to shift in the darkness of an alley between the post office and the grocer's.

I glared in the direction of the shadow.

The longer I stared, the more I convinced myself that I was losing my mind. The shadows were unmoving, and I was wondering if I'd just seen them move out of sheer exhaustion.

I slowly started toward the alley, hoping not to make much noise with each step I took. Perhaps it was nothing more than a cat, or a stray dog. Nevertheless, I still needed to be careful so as not to frighten the poor creature...

But something deep down within me told me that it wasn't an animal. I had *felt* a gaze on my back. It was as if someone had been waiting for me, and had known precisely where I would be this afternoon.

Which makes utterly no sense, I thought. *How could anyone have been able to follow after my footsteps today? I was all over the town.*

Something in the shadows moved once again, which startled me.

Someone is there! Someone is watching me!

"Hello?" I shouted after them, starting after the shadow in a run. I didn't have time to stop and think about how foolish I was being, chasing after this shape, this person.

I plunged into the shadows, and came to a quick stop.

There was no one there.

The dim light of the cloudy day washed the wall up ahead, filtering down through a gap between the buildings.

I stared around, suddenly feeling a great deal more vulnerable than I had before.

Whoever it was had gone. They'd somehow managed to turn a corner before I could catch up.

I took several steps backwards, back out of the alleyway and onto the road, my heart hammering against my ribs.

This felt just like it did the last time. Whoever it had been was now gone. They'd disappeared, just like before.

I turned and started toward the police station once again, wrapping my arms around myself, trying to stop the goose pimples that were appearing on my body.

I'm not crazy, I thought. *I know there was someone there. Just like a few weeks ago.*

This mystery was far too closely tied to the other mystery that had seemed to be following me...the series of break-ins that had been happening at my home.

Both of these incidents had happened twice now. Both times I had not been able to catch whoever it was that was doing it, nor had I been able to find any trace of them, either.

Someone is going to great lengths to hide from me, I thought, my face draining of all color. *And I wonder if it's the same person who was looking for something of mine, breaking into my home as easily as if it were their own place of residence.*

As it always was, my greatest fear was that it had something to do with the murder I was currently investigating. It proved to not be true the last two cases I'd involved myself in, but how could I be sure that someone wasn't following my progress, or hadn't somehow discovered my desire to be involved?

The police station appeared up ahead, and there was no sign of the mysterious, shadowed person following after me. Even if I didn't feel as if whoever it was followed after me now, I still couldn't shake the crawling feeling in my skin as I thought about just how starkly I had been able to feel their gaze upon me.

I saw a group of people gathered out front of the station, and as I drew closer, heard their angry voices all trying to talk over one another.

I recognized Sam Graves' profile from behind the mob, his arms outstretched, and trying to call out over the heads of the other townsfolk.

"Why are we allowing that camp to exist?" I heard an elderly woman shout out as she clung to her walking cane.

"Those Germans could come to the village and kill us all!" said a gentleman that I saw frequently outside of the pub down the street from my cottage.

"Why are the police just sitting here, and not finding out who the article writer is?" asked a woman with an infant strapped to her back.

"Everyone, if you would please wait your turn to be spoken with," Sam shouted over their heads, his hands cupped over his mouth. "The chief only has so much time in his day."

I made my way around the edge of the crowd, the same newspaper I had clutched in my hand being waved in the air by one older gentleman, and stomped underneath the foot of a woman who was probably ten or so years younger than I was.

"Inspector Graves?" I asked, coming toward the front of the group.

Sam's gaze shifted toward me, and immediately I could see that I had picked the wrong time to come and visit him.

"Lightholder..." he said, in a surprisingly informal way. He frowned. "As you can see, I'm very busy."

"I came about this," I said, holding the paper out to him. "But I had some other things to share with you as well. About – "

"Yes, I know what about," he said, cutting me off.

"You're going to talk to her, but not to us?" asked a woman whose skin was so wrinkled it rivaled a currant.

Sam ignored the woman. "Come with me," he said to me, waving me up toward the station doors.

The crowd was none too pleased with the Inspector's decision.

"Tuttle, I need you out here," Sam said, opening the door and leaning in. "Keep them under control while I speak with a consultant."

The man named Tuttle had an impressively thick moustache. "I just came in an hour ago," he said, his equally bushy eyebrows furrowing. "You want me to go back out there?"

"I'll take your night shift next Friday evening," Sam said coolly, his gaze sharp.

Mr. Tuttle's moustache quivered, but he met Sam's stare

easily. "Fine," he said after a moment, getting to his feet. "But you'll take next Friday as well as the night shift after that. I've got a new baby at home and my wife could use the sleep."

Sam stepped aside as Mr. Tuttle walked past him back out onto the landing.

"All right, all right, keep it down," Mr. Tuttle said, putting his hat on his head. "No, Mrs. Myer, the chief isn't ready to see you yet."

Sam jutted his chin toward the door, asking me to follow.

I slipped in the door, Sam following. When he closed it, the quiet that followed was blissful.

"So, consultant, huh?" I asked as we started toward his office at the back of the building. "I hadn't been informed about my promotion."

Sam shot me a sidelong look. "Consultant is a term that we use around here for someone who gives us information for free, so don't flatter yourself," he said. But he still looked down at me, smiling somewhat. "So let me guess...you're here for the same reason that all of those coots outside are? That ridiculous article published in the newspaper this morning?"

I smiled up at him. "Well, well, I can certainly see why you are the inspector, seeing that you have such a keen intuition."

He stopped at the door to his office, pushing the door open. He chuckled, deep in his throat. "Yes, well, I suppose something had to be good enough about me to get the job, right?"

I waited until we were inside and he closed the door behind himself to speak.

"I also wanted to talk to you about Mrs. Lowell," I said. "I think I found out who her secret lover was."

He had reached to pick up some papers, and was just tapping them on his desk to straighten them when my words apparently registered in his mind. He slowly looked up at me, his blue eyes as piercing as they always were. "Did you now?"

I nodded. "The description that Evangeline gave us? It matches a man named Mr. Fenton here in the village. He owns the local bookshop."

I thought it best to make it seem as if I had simply stumbled upon this information like a happy accident, instead of letting it be known that I had shared everything that Evangeline had told us in confidence with Nathanial, Irene, and Sidney that night at dinner.

Sam's eyes narrowed, and my face flushed. Did he know that I was hiding something from him? He was an inspector, after all. His whole profession revolved around discovering the truth about people, and discerning whether or not they were lying to him.

And as lying did not come easily to me...

"I take it you went and investigated it yourself?" he asked, resuming the organization of his papers.

"I did," I said, somewhat relieved that he didn't press to know where I'd learned the information. "I went to visit the bookshop and ran into him, as well as overheard some interesting conversations with some of the customers."

I filled him in on the conversation that Mr. Fenton had with Mrs. Charles, as well as about Tessa Harmon's appearance.

"So Mr. Fenton is likely the man Evangeline believed was Mr. Smith," he said, moving the papers to a drawer in his desk. "And then Miss Harmon's appearance adds another complication."

"Precisely what I thought," I said. "But then that newspaper article appeared, and I was wondering what you might make of all this."

He sighed, laying his palms flat on his desk. "The lack of sense from those editors down at the paper," he muttered underneath his breath. "Why on earth they would ever agree to publish such nonsense..."

"You don't think there is any merit to what the writer said?" I asked.

Sam sighed, standing up straight once again, and reaching for his hat on the hat stand behind his desk. "No," he said. "But that doesn't mean I can dismiss it so readily. I don't have any choice but to go and investigate the claims that were made, even if we don't know if the writer has any sort of authority in this matter."

I blinked at him. "You don't know who wrote the article?"

Sam rubbed his forehead, and paused to look over at me. "Are you saying you do?"

"Oh, no," I said, shaking my head. "No, not at all. I just assumed you would by now."

His stern look morphed into a grimace. "Unfortunately, the charming owner of the newspaper refuses to let me know his sources, saying it would be a breach of contract. As you can imagine, we around here find that rather infuriating."

"I certainly can imagine," I said.

"Well, as much as I would like to continue to discuss this new information about Mr. Fenton and Miss Harmon, I must be off," he said. "I need to get to that prison camp before it gets much later in the day."

"Perhaps I could go with you," I said.

He stopped in his walk around the desk and gave me a flat look.

My stomach dropped. *Well...I suppose it was worth a try.*

11

"I suppose I could use the trip over to the camp as a chance to discuss this information you brought to me," Sam said, grabbing his coat from the back of the door and shrugging it on. "But if you do come, then you have to realize where I am going."

"To the prison camp, I know," I said, getting to my feet.

"And you know who they house there, right?" Sam asked, straightening the collar of his jacket.

"The German prisoners of war, correct?" I asked.

He nodded. "Indeed. Are you certain that's where you want to go, given your history?"

Once again, I was taken aback by Inspector Graves' kindness. He certainly was more sensitive than I gave him credit for...or what his usual manner made him seem like.

"I'll be all right," I said, putting on a smile.

As we walked through the station together, though, my heart ached somewhat. How would I handle being around these men who were fighting alongside those that had killed my husband?

What if some of them were the men who had been flying the planes that dropped the bombs over London that night? What if one of them there was the man who was responsible for Roger's untimely end?

I pushed those thoughts away, knowing they were fruitless, and would do nothing except torment me when there was no possible way of knowing the truth.

I noticed the looks that some of the other officers were giving us as we walked through the station. I saw skepticism, surprise, and even hostility. I ducked my head, wondering if, once again, I'd pushed myself too far into a situation that had nothing to do with me.

The crowds outside the station were still gathered there, and the cacophony of their voices greeted us as soon as Sam walked outside.

"Inspector," said the gangly officer who had somehow taken over from Tuttle in the last few moments. "I could really use a hand here – "

Sam didn't cease his descent down the stairs toward the cars. "I'm sorry, Mable, but I have other matters that need to be attended to tonight."

Mr. Mable's gaze swept over to me, and his brow creased. "Are you two stepping out to dinner?" he asked.

Sam lifted an eyebrow. "I'm going to pretend I didn't hear anything so foolish, Mable. Now get back to those crowds. Do your job."

Mable nodded, and turned his attention back to his work.

I hurried after Sam as he continued on to the car.

I didn't say a word as he started the engine and we pulled out of the parking space. Two of the protestors came up to the window, and began to bang on the glass with their fists, staring angrily inside.

Sam ignored them completely and eased the car onto the road.

"I'm sorry about that..." he said after a few moments of driving in silence. "Mable never should have assumed something so foolish."

"It's all right," I said.

"Not that dinner with you would be foolish, mind," he added hastily. I noticed spots of color appearing in his cheeks. "I imagine it would be quite nice, and – " he cleared his throat loudly, his eyes firmly fixed on the road in front of him.

Color rose in my own face, much to my surprise. How had this conversation even come about?

"Anyway..." Sam said, the gravelly note in his voice returning. "I realized that it was best to let you come along with me this time, simply because I knew that you would likely try to go all the way out there on your own anyways. I would rather be with you so I can be around if anything goes awry."

"Awry?" I asked. "What could possibly go awry?"

A smirk appeared on his face as he looked sidelong over at me. "With you? I imagine the worst possible case scenarios."

The color in my face deepened in anger. "Oh, really?"

"It's just your way, Helen," he said. "Look at Mrs. Martin. And then with everything that happened up at the Cooke farm. I think it would be easier if I were there already in case something did happen."

"It's as if you're assuming that some of the soldiers are

going to break free from their confinement and come and find me," I said, still glaring up at him.

"Perhaps nothing that extreme, but nevertheless, if you are going to be investigating this case, then allow me to help. That's all I'm saying," he said.

I knew deep down that I was wounded because he was, in fact, correct about what would have happened if he hadn't let me go along to the camp. I likely would have gone out there all the way on my own, under some guise that was entirely made up.

He was also correct that trouble seemed to find me wherever I went. I wasn't sure what it was about my move to Brookminster, but it seemed that ever since I arrived, my ability to attract unwanted problems was only ever increasing.

"Are you all right?" he asked. "You've become rather quiet."

"I'm fine," I said, perhaps a bit too sharply. "I think you're right, you know," I added a moment later, in a gentler tone. "Trouble does seem to follow me around."

"You aren't the only one," Sam said. "I've had my fair share of it as well over the years. There are just some people who unfortunately are created to be able to handle it better, and we are the ones who end up seeing the world for what it really is."

I pondered his words as we made our way outside of town, through the rolling countryside. Despite the looming rain overhead, and the darkening skies, sheep were still out in the vibrant green hills, their only concern being whether or not to eat the grass where they stood, or whether the grass nearer their friend was better.

The camp was further outside the village than I expected. As promised, Sam asked me about Mr. Fenton and Miss Harmon, and I gave him the account of what I'd seen once again in detail.

"I'll go and speak with Mr. Fenton, but something tells me this is going to lead to yet another dead end," Sam said. "Which is frustrating, since I had hoped this Mr. Smith would be the one to help us unravel everything, given the secretive tendencies of Mrs. Lowell."

"Well, perhaps he still might," I said. "And he might be able to tell you more about Miss Harmon as well."

"A jilted lover is nothing new," Sam said.

"Yes, but the way she despised poor Mrs. Lowell, it simply makes me wonder if – "

My thoughts died away as we crested a hill...and found a fortress nestled at the foot of a steep knoll.

It looked far more like a permanent structure than a camp, or a farm, despite its large size. High fences encircled the entire plot of land. There were tents and military vehicles all throughout, as well as small huts that looked more stable. Fields spanned out on all sides of the compound, likely where the prisoners were put to work every day.

When we approached the farm, we found a checkpoint, along with a gate, before we were even able to cross into the perimeter.

The soldiers standing guard at the gate held their rifles, and looked none too pleased about a visitor.

One of the soldiers approached the car. He couldn't have been older than twenty, perhaps twenty-one.

Sam rolled down the window of the car.

"Name and business?" the soldier asked.

"Inspector Graves of the Brookminster police," Sam said. "I'm here on an investigation."

The soldier at the car straightened and looked over at a corresponding guard beside the gate. It was as if they were having a silent conversation before he bent back down to look at Sam. "And her?" he asked, nodding toward me.

Sam glanced over at me. "My stenographer," he said. "I need her to transcribe my conversations, as well as utilizing her as a witness."

The soldier shifted on his feet, looking down at his boots. He sighed, but didn't protest the inspector's words. "Badge?" he asked.

Sam obliged, pulling his out from his front pocket. He showed it to the soldier.

The soldier took a step back from the car, and gave a signal to the gate keeper. Two soldiers moved to part the gates, and stood aside to allow our car through.

We entered a road that likely would have led to the farm at one point in time, but now was lined with wire fences that were topped with barbed wire coils.

Peering through the fences, I saw there were tents and huts that were surrounded by even more fencing.

"You cannot look in any direction without seeing a soldier," I said.

"Indeed," Sam said. "This place is well protected. It's been some time since I've been up here to see the progress of things. It appears to have grown since I was here last."

At the end of the road, we were approached by another soldier, who directed our car off to the side of the farmhouse, which seemed to be working as the camp's headquarters.

As I stared around at all of the security, I wondered if

this was simply a fruitless errand for us. How could anyone escape a place like this?

We were escorted to the front porch of the charming home, which had a porch swing and a pair of terracotta planters that looked as if their flowers had seen much better days. We were quickly rushed over the threshold, which made me rather sad. This house used to belong to a family, and likely had many happy memories attached to it. How had a home so lovely fallen into use as a prison camp?

There were just as many soldiers inside the house as we were led back through the narrow front hall, past a darling sitting room decorated in yellows, and back into a home study nearer the back of the house.

The soldier leading us knocked on the door.

"Who is it?" asked a nasally voice from behind the door.

"There is an Inspector Graves here to see you, sir," said the soldier.

The sound of something being slammed down greeted us, as well as the sharp scraping noise of a chair being pushed back.

The door was yanked open a moment later, and a sour looking bald man with a greying moustache and sharp brown eyes stood before us.

"What do you want, Graves?" the man asked.

Sam, who stood nearly a head taller than the man, didn't flinch in the slightest. "Sergeant Crow," he said. "How nice to see you again."

"I certainly do not agree," Sergeant Crow said. "What in the world are you doing here so late? It's very nearly eight o'clock. Come back tomorrow during more reasonable hours."

He brushed past us both.

Sam gave me a dark look, and pursued the Sergeant down the hall.

"I think you know why I'm here, Sergeant," Sam said as we followed him into what looked like a dining room, but had more recently been converted into a meeting room. Maps stretched across the walls, tacked haphazardly into place, and filing cabinets stood on either side of the cherry curio cabinet, which still held pretty china.

"To be perfectly honest, Inspector, I couldn't care less why you are here," the Sergeant said, snatching a manila file off the table, giving Sam the briefest of glances before turning right back around and heading toward the office.

"I understand that you wouldn't want this whole business to reflect badly on you," Sam said, following after the Sergeant as if we'd been asked to. "Truly, I do. But I have every reason to believe that the article published in the newspaper was nothing more than the rantings of some nervous person who – "

"Well, then why did you need to come all the way out here, then, hmm?" Sergeant Crow asked, his dark eyebrows bent in a V shaped crease across his tall forehead. "If the whole thing is false, then you are doing nothing more than wasting my time."

"You know very well that I have to do my due diligence and follow up, just as you would have to if you were in my shoes," Sam said. "I am here on authority, as you know. I am simply doing my job."

The Sergeant glared up at Sam. "You do realize that this article has already invoked the wrath of my superiors?" he asked. "I received a call before noon about the accusations of the lack of security around here. It was stated that if any of these things ended up being even remotely true, that many of us here might be discharged. Can you imagine what that would do to my men? To their families?"

It pleased me to see some humanity within the Sergeant. These men had lived through a great deal, and it was no wonder that he'd become as hardened as he was. Nevertheless, it soothed my nerves ever so slightly to hear that he cared about the men under his command.

"I understand that," Sam said. "Which is part of the reason why I came here. My hope is to verify that these accusations are false, and to do that I am going to need to speak with some of the inmates."

The Sergeant leaned forward on his desk, much in the same way Sam had back at his office. Two men in similar roles, both carrying great burdens.

He looked up at Sam, his eyes narrowing. "I suppose you can speak to a few of them," he said. "Though I'm not sure what you will be able to discern from them."

"Leave that to me," Sam said.

The Sergeant finally glanced over at me. "And who is this that you've brought with you? I'm surprised you would have brought a lady to such an unsafe place."

"She's my stenographer," Sam said. "I am hoping to get some direct statements from the inmates to use in a rebuttal article tomorrow morning."

"I see," Sergeant Crow said. "Very well, she may observe your conversations, but she is not to sit with you in the same room as the prisoners."

"I agree," Sam said, looking over at me. "It wouldn't be safe."

"She can, however, follow with us, and I will take her to

the observation area," Sergeant Crow said. "I hope you are both ready for a tedious evening. Translating for these soldiers has proven...well, cumbersome."

"We can be patient," Sam said. "You need not worry about us."

12

The Sergeant led us through the parts of the camp where the soldiers would travel. We learned that most of the prisoners were from Germany, but there were also some Ukrainians, and even one French soldier who had deserted his own troops.

"And what do they do all day?" I asked as we walked toward one of the more substantial looking buildings that had been constructed.

"Work," Sergeant Crow said. "Out in the fields, mostly. They're all watched over by armed guards, though, to ensure they don't run."

"Every soldier is watched at all hours of the day?" Sam asked.

Sergeant Crow nodded. "There are always several sets of eyes on each group of prisoners."

I jotted that down on the small notepad, just like I had when we had visited Evangeline. The possibility that one of the soldiers had somehow slipped away and killed Mrs. Lowell was becoming less and less likely by the moment.

We entered the building, which was significantly cooler than the outside, despite the chill in the air already, as the sun had now likely set. It was bare, sterile, and depressing. No art hung on the walls, and there was no color aside from the drab grey of the walls and the floor.

"This way," the Sergeant said.

He directed us down another hall lined with doors, all of which had sizable locks on them. A chill crawled up my arms. Was this where they kept the prisoners?

"In here," Sergeant Crow said. "This is where you can watch the interrogations, Miss...?"

"Lightholder," I said, choosing the truth as opposed to making up a name.

"Lightholder?" the Sergeant repeated, his thick eyebrows furrowing once again.

For a moment, I thought for certain that he was going to say something about knowing Roger, and my heart jumped into my throat.

The moment passed, though, and he showed me inside.

It was a cramped space, and very dark. The right wall, however, was mostly taken up by a thick, glass window. It didn't look outside. Instead, it peered into the room beside it, which was just as barren as the rest of the building. There was nothing in there apart from a metal table, and two chairs positioned on either side.

The interrogation room.

"Wait here," Sergeant Crow said. "I'll take Inspector Graves – "

"One moment," Sam said.

He gently laid a hand on my shoulder and guided me over to the corner of the room. Bending his head lower, he whispered to me.

"Just take down whatever seems relevant, all right?" he asked. "I think we both know how this is going to end tonight, but if there is even a chance that one of these men here killed Mrs. Lowell..."

I nodded. "I agree. It's best if we're thorough."

He nodded as well and straightened. "I won't be able to communicate with you through the glass," he said. "But if you see me...oh, I don't know...let's say rest my hand on my cheek, and tap my finger three times, I want you to pay extra attention to what the prisoner is saying."

"Very well," I said. "I will watch for that."

Sergeant Crow grabbed one of the soldiers from the hall to stand inside with me and guard the door, and then guided Sam back out into the hall.

I let out a heavy sigh, wrapping my arms around myself to maintain some of the heat being leeched from my body in that cold room.

The door on the other side of the glass opened a few moments later, and Sergeant Crow showed Sam inside.

Sam didn't appear uneasy in the least, even though he was about to be speaking with some of the country's enemies. He took the seat on the right, adjusting his tie.

"I'll go get the prisoners lined up," Sergeant Crow said.

His voice came through a little speaker set into the corner of the room. It made it sound as if I was hearing him through the receiver on my telephone at home.

"Make sure they're unbiased choices, Sergeant," Sam said. "I need to make sure."

Sergeant Crow studied Sam for a moment, but nodded, and disappeared out the door once again.

Sam then turned to the glass. "You all right in there, Lightholder?"

I nodded, and then realized that he couldn't see me.

"There's a communication box right there," said the soldier who was guarding the door on my side. He pointed to a small, metal square with a red button on it.

I walked over to it and pressed the button. "Yes, I'm just fine," I said, and then released the button.

He nodded. "Good. We will get the information we need, and then I'll make sure that we get back to the station."

I swallowed, my throat becoming tight. This was not at all how I had expected my day to go. It was starting to seem like several days, given the level of exhaustion I was beginning to feel, especially in my knees and my head.

But I didn't want my weakness to show, so I stood straight in front of the glass, my notepad poised in my hand, ready to be written upon.

It wasn't long before the door on the opposite wall opened, and two soldiers entered with a third man who was handcuffed between them.

The soldiers deposited him in the chair across from Sam.

He was young. I wasn't sure why I expected to find someone who was much older, as most of the soldiers who were walking around through the camp here were young, as well. He couldn't have been older than a teenager.

Another man stepped into the room, dressed in a brown suit, and stood off to the side.

It took a moment for the soldiers to get the prisoner situated, but when he was, he simply sat there, staring across at Sam with a look of curiosity and distaste.

Sam glanced at the man in the brown suit. "I assume you are the translator?"

The man nodded. "Yes. I am Mr. Bower." He held out his

hand to Sam. There was a distinct accent in his words, and I couldn't quite place it.

"Inspector Graves," Sam said, shaking. He then nodded toward the prisoner. "And who is joining us this evening?"

"This is Johan Schneider," said Mr. Bower. "He was captured about six months ago, brought straight here when he attempted to infiltrate the border."

It was hard to imagine someone like him trying to cross over into England, likely searching for information. Maybe he would be good to question, given his abilities and skills for espionage and stealth.

Sam cleared his throat, turning to the young man.

Johan likely couldn't understand what was being spoken between the two men, yet he looked back and forth expectantly.

"Mr. Schneider...good evening, my name is Inspector Graves. I have some questions that I would like you to answer. They are not for you, specifically, but about all of the prisoners here at the camp."

He waited as Mr. Bower quickly rattled off his translation to the young prisoner in German.

Johan nodded, and responded, maintaining eye contact comfortably with the inspector.

"He says that he will answer your questions," said Mr. Bower.

"Very good," Sam said. "There are claims that one of the prisoners here at the camp somehow managed to escape and made his way to the nearest village some miles from here."

He waited as it was translated, and Johan responded.

"He says that he has no knowledge of anyone escaping

this place," said Mr. Bower. "And he says that he himself has never tried."

"I would certainly believe that," said the soldier behind me in a low voice.

I glanced over my shoulder at him. "What do you mean?"

"Johan is one of our best behaved prisoners," said the soldier with a shrug. "He never complains, never argues, always does what he is told precisely when he is told to do it..." He shifted on his feet, adjusting his grip on his rifle. "Which is why he always has us so on edge. Why is he so complacent? It just feels rather unnatural is all."

I looked back at the room, studying Johan's face more closely, managing to catch the tail end of Sam's next question.

" – and claims that one of the prisoners managed to kill a local woman while away from the camp. If such a person remained at large, some might think that his entire disappearance was covered up to conceal a hole in the security of this camp," Sam said, arching an eyebrow as he studied Johan as intently as Johan studied him.

Johan listened to the translation, shook his head, and leaned back in his seat, his hands still outstretched on the table, locked in place. He answered, his voice calm, and the translator listened.

"He says that no one here would attempt escape," said Mr. Bower. "He says it is impossible."

I frowned. This young man seemed to be giving us the answers we wanted to hear. Wouldn't it be easier to believe that all of these soldiers were good prisoners, did as they were told, and caused no trouble? If they behaved, then would they be released as soon as the war was over? Were they simply biding their time?

After some time, it was clear that Johan's responses were not going to change. He kept saying that no one had escaped, and that no one could escape.

"He's not wrong, you know," said the blonde soldier in the room with me. "No one could escape from here. Not ever."

I glowered at the glass. I wondered how pleased Sergeant Crow would be with this soldier for being as flippant as he was.

Sam pulled a photo out from his pocket, which startled me. Even from this distance, it was clear that it was a photo of Mrs. Lowell. I had seen it in the papers beside her obituary. It was remarkable just how much she looked like her daughter, with the same feathery, pale blonde hair, narrow face, and round, beautiful eyes.

"Do you recognize this woman?" Sam asked.

Johan leaned forward, peering at the image.

I watched his face closely, searching for any hint of change; a narrowing of the eyes, a twitch of the mouth. Yet nothing happened.

Johan sat up straight, and shook his head. "No," he said, directly to Sam.

I wondered if it was the only English word he knew.

Sam soon sent Johan away, his shoulders sagging as soon as he was out of the room. "There was no point in continuing to speak with him," Sam said, glancing over at the glass. "He was saying the same thing over and over again. We weren't going to get anywhere."

I walked over to the speaker, and pressed the button

down. "I was getting the same feeling. I'm concerned he was telling you what you wanted to hear."

Sam nodded. "I was thinking the same thing."

There was a loud buzzer, and the door across from Sam opened once again, and another soldier was brought in.

"The trouble is that it's incredibly hard to know whether or not they are answering the questions truthfully," the soldier behind me said. "These men have been trained to keep their expressions neutral, regardless of the questions that are asked. Even a man as intimidating as the Inspector there wouldn't be able to frighten them."

I chewed on the inside of my cheek, biting back a retort. The soldier was right, after all, and I bristled because his words were striking a fear head on. What if they were lying to Sam? What if this whole trip was a waste of time, and we would have nothing more than these prisoners' false words to return with? We would still be at the starting line, still wondering if it was at all possible that one of them had snuck off the camp and killed Mrs. Lowell.

Sam asked this prisoner the same questions he'd asked Johan. Had anyone broken out? Might anyone have somehow made it to the village? Did they recognize the woman in the photo?

The prisoner answered no to them all, as did the following four prisoners that were brought in to be questioned.

Every question that was answered with yet another no made Sam even more antsy. First the wrinkles in his forehead deepened. Then his leg began to bounce. As they escorted the sixth prisoner from the room, his hands were both balled into fists and there were patches of deep red all over his face and neck.

"I think your inspector is simply fighting a losing battle," the soldier behind me said, once again unsolicited. "It might be better to just give up."

Was he some sort of mind reader? Why was it that he continued to say all of the things that were passing through my own mind?

I walked over to the communication box, and pressed my palm against it. "We could sit here all night, Sam, but this is not getting us anywhere."

Sam, who was pacing back and forth behind the table, massaging his temples, stopped. He looked up at the glass. "Every one of them was lying to me," Sam said. "I don't know about what, but it is quite obvious they were all trained very well. Each and every one of them."

"I know," I said. "What should we do?"

Sam glared down at the floor, rubbing the back of his thick neck. "We leave," he said, holding his hands out in defeat. "We don't have any other choice, do we?"

*No, we don't...*I thought. These men would likely continue to give us these same answers no matter how long we stayed.

We apologized to the Sergeant a short while later. As I glanced at the clock on his wall, I realized that it was after midnight.

"Well, you got what you needed, right?" he asked. "None of these men escaped. You can squash those rumors now."

"If I trusted what they were saying to me, I certainly would," Sam said. "But I'm not sure I can rely on what they said."

Sergeant Crow was none too pleased with that response. "Inspector, I appreciate your willingness to come all the way out here, but I can assure you...without a doubt...that this camp has the highest security possible. No one has ever escaped, and no one will. Not as long as I am in charge of this operation. If you cannot take the words of the prisoners, then take mine. I trust the soldiers in my command to be vigilant and of sound mind at all times while they are serving here. The moment I see any lax behavior, *the very moment*...I ship them out of here back to London."

Sam nodded. "Very well, Sergeant. I have no reason to doubt you. You can consider those rumors extinguished, and the reputation of your camp safe."

"Thank you," Sergeant Crow said, rather heavily. "And you do your part to ensure that the good people of Brookminster do not lose sleep over such a ridiculous article."

"I will do my best," Sam said.

We departed a short time later, making our way back through the fenced drive, passing through the gate, and onto the road headed back into town.

"I'm sorry to have wasted your night," Sam said.

"No need to apologize," I said. "I suppose we can rule out these prisoners as suspects now, can't we?" I asked.

Sam's expression hardened. "...I suppose we can."

The reluctance on his face was telling me a different story.

13

The rest of the way home, Sam and I redirected our attention back to Mrs. Douglas, the landlady, Mr. Fenton the bookshop owner, and Miss Harmon.

"To be honest, Mrs. Douglas has been canceling – no, pardon me, *rescheduling* – our meeting together all this week," Sam said, shaking his head. "Every time I try to call her at home, she never answers. I've even gone by there on my way home from the station in the evenings, and she simply never seems to be there."

"Do you think she's avoiding you because she is the one who killed Mrs. Lowell?" I asked.

He sighed, rubbing his face. "I'm not entirely sure. Yes, Mrs. Douglas certainly seems like she could be the sort of woman with a personal vendetta against someone like Mrs. Lowell. After speaking to her neighbors, it's clear that the two women did not get along very well. When Mrs. Lowell needed a place to stay after her husband died, she did very little to fulfill her end of the agreement, which was to pay Mrs. Douglas rent every four weeks. From what I was told,

Mrs. Douglas was initially very kind about the price, saying the widow could pay half what her other tenants had to until she was able to get back on her feet…"

We drove past the sign welcoming us back into Brookminster, the light from the streetlamps along the road dispelling the darkness that only nearly one in the morning was familiar with.

"It seems that Mrs. Lowell did nothing to help herself, though. She spent much of her days holed up in her house, while litter and dirty dishes built up. Her daughter was often heard to visit her friends in the evenings, just so she could have some dinner to bring back to her mother."

"She was grieving, from the sound of it," I said.

"Yes, but even still, there is a point where the grief must be set aside, and life lived once again," Sam said. "It seems that Mrs. Douglas gave her many chances to set the situation right, even forgiving several months worth of rent in the hopes that it would encourage Mrs. Lowell to pick herself back up…but it seems like it never happened."

I frowned, staring down at my hands knit together in my lap. "She allowed the grief to completely take over."

"Precisely," Sam said. "So, naturally, Mrs. Douglas became angry with her, which is not entirely unreasonable. She does have bills to pay, her own family to care for. Grace for others who have experienced such terrible loss is all well and good, but coddling people is not. It's simply debilitating. And Mrs. Douglas wasn't going to do that, which I assume is why Evangeline told us they fought as much as they did."

"I imagine so, yes," I said. "But didn't Evangeline also say Mrs. Douglas was being rather hostile, by shutting the water off and kicking them out to have repairs done?"

Sam sighed. "We must remember that these stories were

all told from the perspective of a child. A young child, no less. We must take what she said with a grain of salt, and perhaps realize that her love for her mother and her desire to see someone brought to justice might be altering her memories of those events ever so slightly."

I thought back to the house, and how dilapidated it was. "I wonder if the house's poor condition was Mrs. Lowell's doing, and not Mrs. Douglas's like I had thought."

"It very well could have been," Sam said. "If she was neglecting it for months, so absorbed in herself that she didn't even notice the disrepair...and if Mrs. Douglas simply wanted to ensure that the house was still in working order for them while she waited for Mrs. Lowell to come out of her stupor."

I exhaled sharply through my nose. "There truly are two sides to every story."

"Now, this business with Miss Harmon," said Sam slowly as we turned onto High Street. All of the houses stood quietly in their rows, all of the windows dark. "I know this woman. And from what you have explained to me, you do not. Allow me to tell you who Miss Tessa Harmon actually is..."

He slowed to a stop outside of my house, turning the bright headlights off so as to not disturb any of my neighbors, including Sidney, whose home was right beside my own.

"That woman is a terrible gossip, but she is a great deal more like a snarling dog without any teeth," Sam said. "I wish I could tell you the number of times I've heard that woman complaining about someone else, or flippantly talking in public about how much she despised someone... People have accused her of all kinds of things; theft, forgery, defamation – though that last one is true – and all of them have landed her in my office at one time or another," he said. "I have to keep telling her to realize when it's time to keep her mouth shut."

Irene had said much the same. "Is there anyone in this world she does like?" I asked.

Sam laughed, which startled me. "Of course," Sam said. "Men. And she moves from interest to interest as easily as if she were changing her shoes. She even made an attempt to woo me once."

My eyes widened. "You?"

He looked at me, arching an eyebrow. "You can see how successful she was at that," Sam said. "My point is that she might be interested in Mr. Fenton this week, but it is quite possible that come next week, she will be moving her advances on to someone else. She likes a challenge. As soon as Mr. Fenton starts to show any interest in return, she will forget him."

"I see," I said. That certainly did seem to fit her character type. When Mr. Fenton was flat out refusing her charms at the bookshop, it seemed to only encourage her further.

"It's quite masochistic, isn't it?" I asked. "Only engaging with someone who is not interested?"

"It certainly is," Sam said. "Now, this Mr. Fenton, you said he's the one that owns the bookshop, yes? Quiet? Nervous all the time?" he asked.

"Yes," I said. "I've even heard that he is terribly accident prone. Some say he's cursed."

Sam rolled his eyes. "Cursed... The things people in this village believe," he muttered. "The man isn't cursed, he just has the worst luck I've ever seen." He grunted. "I don't believe in luck, either. Look, all I'm saying is that the man has a difficult time not harming himself. He doesn't pay attention to his surroundings, from what I've heard, and he is quite careless. He has been the one to call the police station for help more than anyone else in this town. I hardly ever answer the call, because everyone around the station just knows him as The Catastrophe."

"That's not very kind," I said, frowning.

Sam shrugged.

"He seemed like a perfectly nice man when I met him," I said. "A bit nervous, as you said, but still very amiable."

"Yes, but sometimes the quietest and kindest are the ones that we have to pay special attention to," Sam said.

"Oh come now," I said, glowering at him. "You cannot tell me there is any truth to the idea that it's the quiet ones who are always the troublemakers."

"There certainly is," Sam said. "They are often the ones who are lost under the radar, who everyone looks over."

"He just doesn't strike me as a murderer," I said.

"Sometimes they don't," Sam said. "But emotions running high can push people to do unexpected things. Crimes of passion, you know. They're a real thing."

I wasn't sure how to respond.

"Besides, Evangeline was the one who told us that she overheard them fighting a great deal, right?" Sam said.

"Yes, but I thought that was because Mrs. Lowell felt so guilty about falling in love with someone so soon after her husband died," I said. "I wonder if Mr. Fenton and Mrs. Lowell were friends before her husband passed away."

"I imagine they had to have been," Sam said. "I highly doubt a perfect stranger would want to propose to someone in the state that she was in unless he already had some feelings for her in the first place."

"I would have bypassed him entirely," I said. "He just seemed so broken up over her death."

"A good cover," Sam said. "Deters suspicion away from him. No matter, though. I will be following up with both of these new leads, first thing in the morning if I have any say in it."

He glanced out the window at the still street, and a rumble of thunder echoed far off in the distance.

"I'm sorry that you weren't able to get more concrete answers from those prisoners tonight," I said.

He shook his head. "It's all right. I had expected as much. It's hard to know whether or not it's safe to trust an enemy, after all."

He cleared his throat.

"I shouldn't keep you any longer, Mrs. Lightholder," he said. "I must admit, though, I was appreciative of your company this evening."

I smiled at him, finding once again that I was surprised by his actions. "I'm glad you invited me along."

One of his thick, dark brows arched, and a smile appeared. "I was under the impression that you invited yourself...as you so often seem to do."

Sheepish, I felt my face flush.

"Well, have a good rest of your evening, Mrs. Lightholder," Sam said. "Whatever might be left of it."

"You as well, Inspector Graves," I said.

I stepped out of the car, letting the door close behind me. I waved at him as he pulled along down the road into the night, the pools of light illuminating the car as it went.

It was strange, in a way, having spent an entire evening like that with Sam. And he'd been perfectly pleasant. It certainly wasn't the sort of social outing that I was used to, but it was intriguing to see Sam working the way he was. I was not surprised by his gruffness, nor his cool approach to interrogation.

What had surprised me, though, was his gentleness toward me. There was a caring gentlemen beneath that hard exterior, and I was pleased that I was beginning to see that in him.

I let myself into the house, and found that my heart was light, despite what had happened that evening.

Am I beginning to grow? I thought as I brushed my hair out of its updo, already dressed in my pajamas, my eyelids becoming heavy. *Am I finally starting to move on from Roger?*

I wasn't certain about what, exactly, I might be feeling for Sam. In a way, it was very similar to the sort of comfortableness I felt with Sidney.

They were both very handsome, single men. If I had never met Roger, I would have been thrilled to have found either of them. Both might have made good matches for me.

I shook my head as I shut off the light in my washroom, and made my way into the bedroom. *There is no reason why I should be thinking about either of them like that,* I said to myself. *Neither of them has even shown any interest in me.*

I crawled into my cool, soft bed, pulling the blankets up to my shoulders.

No, it's better if I forget I ever thought about that, I pondered. *Better for me to just protect myself.*

I dozed off that night, and for the first time in a long, long time...I didn't dream about Roger.

14

The next few days passed by without so much as a peep from Sam. I half expected him to call me and let me know what his investigations unearthed, but never heard a thing.

I realized that we must be back at square one, and that both of those leads must have come up empty.

It was rather discouraging, thinking about having to start over completely with the investigation about Mrs. Lowell's murder.

The rest of the village seemed curious about the case as well. I heard more than one person come into my shop, murmuring under their breath about Mrs. Lowell and what had happened to her.

"It's troubling, you know," said Mrs. Trent to me as she paid for a hat that I had redecorated with a brand new ribbon around the peak. "Wondering who this person might be who killed her."

I set her new hat into one of the hat boxes that I had also repurposed, having painted and adorned it with some spare sequins that had fallen off a gawdy dress that had once belonged to my aunt. "I know for certain that Inspector Graves is working very hard on the case," I said. "He is determined to find whoever committed this crime, so that everyone in town can sleep better at night."

Mrs. Trent nodded, but the wrinkles in her forehead told me she was far from consoled. "I hope he is, because yesterday I saw him giving a ticket to Mr. Michaels on his bicycle. Apparently he had parked it in the wrong place."

My face flushed, wondering what on earth he could have been doing. "Well, I suppose the police have many jobs, don't they? Even if there is a murder case to be dealt with, they still must ensure the law is upheld elsewhere."

"I suppose..." Mrs. Trent said. "To be honest, I'm beginning to wonder if there even is a murderer."

"What do you mean?" I asked, pausing as I tied a thick, red ribbon around the box.

"Well, what if no one killed her, but she in fact, took her own life?" Mrs. Trent asked.

Goosepimples popped up on my arms as I finished tying the ribbon and pushed the box across the counter to her. "I'm sure that would have been rather clear from the police investigation," I said.

"But the article said that she was simply found dead in her home, by that young daughter of hers, no less... How can we be certain the child would have even understood what was happening?"

That was a valid point. Had Sam even considered it?

Of course he would have. He had been doing this for many more years than I had. He had more training than I ever would. Surely he would have been able to tell a suicide from a murder?

"Inspector Graves will get down to the bottom of it," I said. "I'm certain of it."

Mrs. Trent gave me a sharp look. "You are quite quick to come to his aid and defend him," she said, a glint in her eye. "I wonder why that might be?"

The color in my face deepened. "It's nothing," I said quickly. "I just know that Sam is very capable, and always does his job to the best of his – "

"Sam?" Mrs. Trent interrupted. "On a first name basis now, are we?"

I wasn't sure why this woman's remarks were so easily getting under my skin, but I managed to keep a smile on my face. "It's nothing, I assure you. I hope you have a pleasant day today, Mrs. Trent."

She paid me, and started out of the shop.

I turned and pretended to go through a box of miscellaneous glass beads I had, dropping the fake smile. She had somehow managed to hit the nail right on the head. Were Sam and I too familiar with one another? And would Mrs. Trent now go and tell others about my familiarity with him?

What in the world would he think of me if anything like that were to reach him? He would think I started it, that I was going around telling everyone we were so friendly with one another.

Appalled, I tried not to think about it. I was likely reading too much into the exchange. Mrs. Trent was a very pleasant woman. I always enjoyed serving her when I worked with Irene at the teahouse. She wasn't the sort to go around and start rumors.

I had to be careful though, now, didn't I? Perhaps it would be unwise for me to be so utterly familiar with Sam. It might come back and harm his reputation. Or mine.

I thought of his words the night before, how he'd been pleased that I had gone with him...

I shook my head, clearing it of those thoughts. It wouldn't do to dwell on them, especially not when there were so many people who might misinterpret things.

I certainly did believe in Sam's skills. I would stand by that. It wasn't my fault that Mrs. Trent saw it in a far more romantic sense than how I had intended it to seem.

The bell over the door at the front chimed, and I turned to see Irene hurry into the shop, a distressed look on her face.

She smiled at Mrs. Georgianna who was standing near the front, looking through some postcards I'd set out, but her smile quickly faded as she hurried toward the back where I was standing.

"Do you have a moment?" she asked. Up close, I could see the fear in her gaze.

"Yes, of course," I said. "Mrs. Georgianna, I'll be right back. I'm just heading upstairs for a few moments."

She gave me a friendly wave in response, and returned her attention to the postcards.

I put up a small sign near the till, saying I was just upstairs and would return momentarily. I then hurried to the back door to my flat, and Irene and I started upstairs.

"What's the matter?" I asked as soon as we reached the landing just inside my kitchen. I closed the door behind her as she hurried inside.

She walked over into the sitting room, and began to pace. "I just overheard something troubling."

"At the teahouse?" I asked.

She looked over at me, nodding. "Yes," she said. "Nathanial overheard it as well, and agreed to watch the shop so I could come and speak to you, and discern whether or not we needed to go to Inspector Graves."

I asked her to sit at the table, and she shook her head.

"It's that serious?" I asked. "Then why didn't you take it right to Sam?"

"Because I wasn't sure if it really was anything more than..." Irene said. "It's Tessa Harmon. She was back in the teashop today."

I nodded. "What happened?"

Irene, wringing her hands, stared blankly at me. "Well, she came into the shop with that friend of hers that she was with last week. They ordered tea, just like last time...and I didn't mean to overhear it, but that woman's voice carries, and she certainly doesn't seem to care if everyone overhears her. I'm not entirely convinced that wasn't her intention in the first place – "

"But what did she say that required you to run all the way over here?" I asked, my heart beginning to beat more quickly.

She sucked in a heavy breath. "She was bragging," Irene said. "About her genius. She said that everyone seemed so utterly convinced that it was that crochety old woman, someone who seemed far more likely than someone who was less connected to her..."

"Did she mention names?" I asked, a knot forming in my chest.

Irene shook her head. "No, and that's why I came over here. We don't know if she meant Abigail, or if she was referring to her landlady...we didn't know. Does this sound like anything that might be of concern?"

She wanted me to say no. She had come all this way not to just tell me, but to have her fears soothed. From her wide-eyed expression, it was clear that she wanted nothing more than for me to dismiss it as nothing, instead of thinking that a possible murderer was sipping tea from her vintage tea set back at her shop.

My shoulders sank, and my heart grew heavy.

"I thought there was something suspicious about her," I said. "From the very beginning..."

"Do you think – " Irene said.

"I'm not positive," I said. "But there is only one way to find out."

15

I t took me almost a quarter of an hour to check out all of the customers that happened to come into the haberdashery while Irene and I were speaking upstairs. I anxiously stood in the back, tapping my fingers impatiently on the counter, kindly asking those who were browsing if they needed any help.

When they didn't seem to want to move, I went and flipped the *Open* sign over, so the *Closed* side was visible outside the door.

"You're closing already?" asked Mrs. Georgianna. "But it isn't even noon yet."

"I'm sorry, but something very important has just come up," I said, loud enough so all of the customers could hear. "If you have anything you wish to purchase, please bring it to the back counter, and I will help you on your way."

It was clear that some of the customers were none too pleased, especially Mrs. Georgianna who likely would have enjoyed staying and looking through every single color of thread that I had recently received in an order.

Finally, the shop closed and the door locked, Irene and I hurried down High Street toward her teahouse.

"She was there when I left," Irene said. "Perhaps she will still be."

"I hope she is," I said.

"Do you intend to talk to her?" Irene asked, the two of us somewhat breathless as we did our best to hurry while still looking inconspicuous.

"I have no idea," I said. "I doubt she would admit anything to me if I was to outright ask her. But if we can maybe catch her talking about it, or if your husband heard anything else…"

The teahouse was bustling when we arrived. Despite the warm, summer morning, people still seemed to want to enjoy their tea and sandwiches.

I gazed around the room as soon as we stepped inside, looking for Tessa Harmon's distinct, dark hair and pink coat. I found neither, however.

"She isn't here," I said.

"But her friend is," Irene said, pointing to the back corner where they had been sitting the first time we had seen them there.

She was correct. Madeline Woods sat at the back table, her head wrapped in a beautiful silk scarf, sunglasses perched on top. She was pouring over what appeared to be a magazine.

"Let's go find Nathanial," Irene said. "He might have overheard something."

I nodded, and together we hurried back to the kitchen.

Nathanial was inside, pouring tea into three ceramic pots. "There you are," he said, setting the kettle down and coming over to Irene. "I wondered if you were all right."

"Everything is fine, dear," she said. "I went and retrieved Helen. Did she say anything else while we were gone?"

Nathanial's face hardened, but he shook his head. "No, nothing else. She never dropped names, but it was clear that something strange was happening. The look on her face... she seemed far too pleased about whatever it was she was bragging about. And to be honest, I'm a little worried about what, exactly, she meant..."

"That's my concern, as well," I said. "And I'm certain that Sam Graves will be interested to hear about it – "

"I'm wondering if taking this to the inspector is the wisest idea," Nathanial said.

"Honey, why?" Irene asked.

"No, I'm sorry...what I meant to say was that I should be the one to go see him," Nathanial said. "I was the one who overheard them in the first place."

"But he has no idea that you are involved in any of this," I said. "It really would be best if you let me go talk to him. I could keep you and Irene out of it completely, so you would never need to be disturbed."

"This is just as much my home as it is yours, Helen," said Nathanial. "I think that we need to stand up and be ready to fight for this village. If Miss Harmon is one of those who is causing trouble...then we need to make sure she answers for it."

Irene laid a hand on her husband's arm.

"I will go speak with him once we close up for the day," Nathanial said. "So you ladies can rest easy. We will get this resolved."

And with that, he lifted the teapots, and carried them back out into the dining room.

Irene sighed, leaning against the counter. She crossed

her arms, frowning. "That husband of mine...I never thought I would worry over a trait that I love so dearly about him."

"What do you mean?" I asked.

"I have always loved his sense of right and wrong. His strong moral core. Now I worry that it might get him into trouble," she said.

"I'm worried about Sam knowing I've dragged you both into this," I said. "He certainly won't be happy with me for being so open with everything."

"It's all right, dear," Irene said. "I'm sure Inspector Graves knows that we aren't the only ones in town discussing it."

"That's for certain," I said, thinking back to Mrs. Trent's comments in the shop earlier that morning.

I crossed to the door and pushed it open a crack, and peered out.

Madeline Woods was still sitting at the table, her foot bouncing as she sipped her tea.

"I wonder if she would be willing to tell us where Tessa lives..." I muttered.

"She might," Irene said.

I glanced over my shoulder at her. "I'm surprised. I expected you to tell me off for thinking it."

She shrank a bit. "Well...If you and my husband are both involved now, then I suppose I cannot stand by and allow you both to stand in harm's way. Besides, whatever information we get could be useful for Nathanial to take to Inspector Graves."

"I'm going with him," I said. "I have no intention of letting your husband speak to the inspector on his own. I know how to speak to him."

"Yes, I've noticed," Irene said.

I noticed the glint in her eyes, but she leaned over me and stared out into the dining room. "Do you still think you want to talk to her about it?" she asked.

"Yes," I said.

"And are you sure that you want to question Tessa?" Irene asked.

"I think so," I said.

"Under what premise?" Irene asked.

"I'll figure that out when we get there," I said, and pushed my way out into the dining room.

Madeline seemed entirely aloof to our presence as we approached the table.

"Hello," I said as kindly as I could.

Madeline looked up at me, slowly, deliberately, a glare in her blue, heavily painted eyes. "No, I don't need any more tea. Thank you."

"My apologies. We aren't here to ask for your order. We had something else to ask you," I said.

Madeline sat back in her chair, still glaring. "Very well."

"There was a woman here with you earlier," Irene said, coming up closer to the table. "We were wondering if you could tell us how we could contact her."

Madeline's eyes narrowed. "Who is asking?" she asked.

"I met her the other day," I said, stepping back in. "And we made plans to have a meeting. She was interested in some of my custom hats."

She snorted. "Your hats? And who might you be?"

I felt Irene's gaze on me, but I smiled easily at Madeline. "My name is Elizabeth Warsaw," I said, using my middle and maiden names. "I'm new to the area. Miss Harmon was kind enough to offer to help me adjust."

Madeline's eyes were no more than slits now. "That

doesn't sound like Tessa," she said. "She never said anything to me about you."

"I don't imagine she would have," I said. "Doesn't Miss Harmon have a great many contacts? Especially those in the fashion world?"

Madeline tossed her hair over her shoulder. "Well, I suppose you are correct about that."

"So you might know where she lives?" Irene asked. "I know Miss Warsaw would appreciate being able to take her stock over to Miss Harmon in person. She is very busy after all. Has to return to London the day after tomorrow."

I knew this was going to come back and haunt me at some point, since this woman lived in town...even though she seemed like the sort of person that I would never spend any time with in the first place.

"Very well," Madeline said. Her lips parted, and she looked suddenly disgusted. "What? Don't you have something to write with? I'm only going to say this once."

Irene fished her notepad from her apron, pencil poised and ready. "Go ahead, Miss Woods. We are all ears."

16

"I never would have expected that she lived over here," Irene said as we stared up at the house that Madeline Woods had assured us belonged to Tessa Harmon.

We were back near the bookshop where Mr. Fenton worked, and about three doors down from Mrs. Lowell's rental house. The cottage itself was quite small, made of the same warm stone that the rest of Brookminster was known for. There was a sizable front garden, with gorgeous, overgrown rose bushes that were in full bloom. A stone fountain stood alongside the path, and a pair of bright yellow birds were bathing in it.

"For some reason, I imagined her in one of the larger homes on High Street," I said. "What did you say she did again?"

"To be honest, I'm not sure," Irene said. "I always thought she owned a shop, but I don't know."

I looked over at Irene, my heart sinking. "You didn't have to come along, you know. I can see that you're worried."

Irene straightened, her brow furrowing. "What do you mean? Of course I had to."

"You didn't," I said. "I know you're worried about Nathanial and Michael."

"They're both just fine," Irene said. "Michael is staying with his cousins for the day, and Nathanial said he was going to go see Inspector Graves as soon as he closed up the teashop, which should be just about any minute now."

"Yet you didn't tell him that we were coming to speak with Tessa," I said.

She frowned. "No, I didn't. And I feel just awful about it."

I laid a hand on her shoulder. "If you want to leave, I will completely understand. I don't want to be a reason why you and your husband fight."

"I will explain everything to him," Irene said. "I should have before we left...but it's all right. I will accept his frustration. But I didn't want to leave you to do this alone, either, Helen. I'm worried about you. He and I both are."

It warmed my heart to hear that. "I appreciate it, Irene. I really do."

I turned my gaze to the house once again, and a chill ran down my spine.

The last time I went to confront a person that I thought was responsible for a murder...she turned on me, and I very nearly died.

I swallowed hard. Perhaps with two of us there, Tessa would be more willing to talk to us.

I wasn't sure, though.

"Let's go," I said, stepping forward.

My heart was racing as we walked up to the front gate of the garden. What was she going to think? What was I going to say?

Even as we walked down the cobblestone path toward the front door, which was painted a soft grey, I still didn't know what I would do.

My throat dry, I stopped before the door.

"Are you all right?" Irene asked. "Maybe it would be best if we went straight to Inspector Graves with this information. Would it be better if he were here to talk to her instead?"

It very well might have been, but something told me that this situation was going to be a great deal like it was with Evangeline, where she would be more willing to talk to me, a nobody, as opposed to the inspector.

I sucked in a breath through my nostrils, and lifted my hand to knock.

"What are you doing here?"

My heart jumped as the voice behind us caught me off guard.

Irene and I turned around and saw Tessa Harmon coming around the outside of her cottage, a pair of glitzy sunglasses over her pale face, her dark hair pulled back in a knot on top of her head.

She certainly was a beautiful woman, able to pull off a swing style swimsuit in a deep, navy blue. It was snug, something far tighter than anything I would be comfortable wearing, even in my own back garden.

She stared at us, her brow furrowing further with every passing moment. "Excuse me, I believe I asked you a question?"

"My apologies," I said. "We were coming to pay you a visit."

One of her perfectly straight eyebrows arched upward,

and her hands went to her hips. "The servers from the teahouse? What could you possibly want with me?"

I took a step toward her, putting some space between her and Irene. "Mrs. Driscoll is one of the owners of the shop. I just work for her when she needs another set of hands," I said. "But more than that, I am – "

"The girl who took over the haberdashery, yes I know," she said, a flash in her gaze. "Did I order something that I forgot about or something? Why does it require the both of you to deliver it, hmm?"

"It certainly doesn't," I said. "I am here for another reason, though. I'm working as a consultant with the police department, and – "

She snorted with derision. "A consultant? Oh, honey, don't flatter yourself. You're telling me that Sam Graves hired *you?*"

I blanched. That was not at all the sort of reaction I had expected. "Well, yes," I said. "I've had experience working on some of the more difficult cases that the police have been – "

"No," she said. "First of all, you're a nobody. Second, There is no way that Sam Graves would ever want the likes of you around."

Anger twinged deep within me. I had expected fury or fear when I'd told her why I was there. But outright mockery?

"If I were you, I would give up on ever trying to get his attention," she said, lifting her sunglasses off her face and tucking them into her dark hair like a crown. "I've been there, done that. The man is a brick wall. Nothing catches his eye. And I can guarantee you that if I wasn't able to get him to turn his head, then you certainly won't."

I gaped at her. She thought this was about competition for him?

"I think you have misunderstood me," I said, a tight smile stretching across my face. "This isn't about Sam."

"Well, that's good," she said. "Because I am *long* over him. You can have him, if you really feel like wasting your time. He'll break your heart. Mark my words."

"I'm quite serious," I said, my voice taking on an edge. "I am a consultant with the police department, and I have come here to ask you about Mrs. Lowell's death."

She was partway through another explanation about Sam Graves' apparent disinterest in anything that wasn't a criminal case, and she froze.

An icy gaze slowly swept over me, and her jaw tightened. "What did you say?" she murmured, a chill in her words to match the frigid glare.

I licked my lips. *There's the anger I expected,* I thought. "We know that you had a connection to Mrs. Lowell, and – "

"I've already spoken with Sam," she snapped, folding her arms. "He already asked me all these questions."

"Yes, but we recently learned about your relationship with Mr. Fenton," I said. "And we know for certain that he had intended to propose to Mrs. Lowell."

A brief flash of fear shone in her eyes, but it quickly disappeared as she scoffed. "I have no relationship with Mr. Fenton. I don't even know who that is."

"Really?" I asked. "We have sources that claim to have seen you with him at his store just a few days ago, making it very clear that you wanted his attention."

"Harmless flirting," she said, turning around on her heel and storming off toward the back of her house.

I didn't wait for her to ask me to follow her. I was getting closer, and the truth pushed me forward. "We also have sources that claim you were discussing Mr. Fenton as well as Mrs. Lowell quite openly over lunch at the teahouse."

She stopped, which caused Irene and I to stop behind her.

Silence followed, and for a moment, I thought she had begun to cry. I wasn't certain, but her whole body was so entirely still that I feared for her.

"Tessa?" I asked.

Her shoulders began to tremble. Low, slow mumbles began to emanate from her.

I took a hesitant step toward her. "Tessa, I – "

She let out a cry of exasperation, wheeling around and pointing at Irene. "This is *your* fault!" she shouted, her voice echoing off the side of her house. "You! You were eavesdropping on me! On my private conversation!"

I threw up my hands, stepping between them once again. "Easy there. It wasn't her. It was someone else who worked there – "

"Then it was *you!*" she said, turning her burning gaze on me, her piercing shriek making me wince.

She moved so fast I barely saw her, but she was up in my face, her nose very nearly touching mine.

"I should have known..." she said. "That one day, the *only* day I had ever seen you at the teahouse working... Madeline and I thought it was strange, the way you kept coming over to our table and checking on us, leaving other tables completely alone. But I never would have thought that you were eavesdropping!"

She prodded me in the chest with her thin, perfectly manicured finger.

"I could have you thrown into jail for stalking," she said,

her words followed by an insidious laugh. "Oh, yes. And don't forget trespassing! You walked onto my property without my permission, and – "

"You have yet to deny my accusations, Miss Harmon," I said. "Were you, or were you not, involved with Mrs. Lowell's death?"

Her chest heaving, she let out an exasperated cry, and turned on her heel.

She started looking around, knotting her hands in her hair, muttering underneath her breath.

"Helen..." Irene whispered behind me.

I glanced over my shoulder.

Irene's face, as pale as milk, was fixed on Tessa. "Something's not right..."

I looked back over at Tessa, who had begun to pace back and forth across her garden. "...never should have found out. I was careful. Incredibly so. That witch Madeline Woods...she dragged it out of me, coerced me – "

"Tessa, why don't you come with me?" I asked, holding my hand out to her. "You can come with me to the police station, where I'm sure that Inspector Graves will want to ask you a few more questions, and – "

"No!"

She ceased her nervous pacing, her gaze like daggers as she glowered at us.

"I didn't do anything – " she said, stooping to pick up a garden trowel that was lying beside a wicker basket near the rose bushes. "I am innocent."

My heart skipped as I watched the slow, deliberate motions she took to stand back to her feet, turning toward us. She gripped the trowel like a knife, and started toward us.

"Tessa," I said, nearly tripping over one of the stones in the path as I walked backward. "Put the trowel down."

"You didn't hear anything...no one did," she said, her gaze distant, her voice mumbled.

"Helen," Irene said sharply. "We need to – "

"Nothing...nothing...nothing," Tessa said, still walking toward us.

I looked around for something to defend myself with. The only thing that I could find was a broom, which was better than nothing.

Just as I reached for it, turning my gaze from her for a fraction of a second, she lashed out at me, the metal of the trowel gleaming in the late morning sun.

I deflected the trowel just in time with the handle of the broom, hoisting it in the air between us.

The force of the collision knocked Tessa off balance, and she staggered backward.

She straightened, her teeth gritted as she glared at me.

"You didn't hear *anything*."

"Freeze!" called another voice.

I whipped around, and my heart leapt into my throat.

Sam Graves stood just on the other side of the low, stone wall surrounding Tessa's garden...his pistol drawn and ready, pointed directly at her.

17

I knew that if I never heard Tessa's pitiful sobs and her attempted bribery ever again, it would be too soon.

As soon as she saw Sam, the trowel had dropped from her hand. She sagged to the ground, her hands trembling, and played the part of the cornered victim incredibly well. She burst into tears, clawing at her face, begging Sam to take me away and punish me for what I had done to her.

I was grateful for Sam's trust in me, because he saw through her outburst as easily as if she were a child.

Two other officers showed up with the police car shortly after, the red light affixed to the roof spinning and flashing.

It only took Sam a few moments to extract the information he needed from her.

Within a quarter of an hour, Tessa Harmon was handcuffed and being loaded into the back of the police car, gnashing her teeth and snarling at the officers to get their hands off of her.

"Well, once again, your instincts appear to have been correct," Sam said as we watched the other two officers climb back into the car, Tessa sobbing hysterically in the backseat. "You were suspicious about Tessa, and I was ready to brush her aside. Perhaps my history with her made it that much easier to do."

There was part of me that wanted to ask him about what sort of history they had, just to hear about how she had thrown herself at him, but I decided to hold my tongue. "Yes, well, if it wasn't for Irene telling me about what she'd overheard this morning at the teahouse – "

Sam looked over the top of my head to Irene, who stood behind me.

"Oh, I'm terribly sorry, Inspector Graves," Irene said. "Please don't be angry with Helen. Nathanial and I were just trying to help her, and – "

Sam nodded. "Yes, your husband is the reason why I'm here," he said. "He came right to the station and told me about Miss Harmon's conversation with Miss Woods. I headed over here as soon as he finished telling me everything."

Irene laid a hand over her heart. "Oh, Nathanial..." she murmured.

"I imagine he won't be too happy to know that you were here," Sam said. "He thought you were back at the teahouse."

Irene flushed. "Yes, I know. I need to go and make things right with him." She looked over at me, smiling, and threw her arms around my neck. "I'm so relieved that you are all right. I was worried you were going to get hurt."

"I'm fine," I said.

"You were very quick thinking, though, reaching for that broom," she said.

She pulled away, her eyes shining with tears. "I have half

a mind to lock you up in my kitchen, you know. That way I will know you are safe."

We laughed, and she stepped away. "I'll call on you later, all right?" she asked.

"Of course, I look forward to it," I said.

She waved as she hurried off, leaving Sam and I standing in Tessa's front garden.

"I will certainly have to question her," Sam said. "But I think it's more important that she has a chance to speak with Nathanial first. Besides, I imagine he told me almost everything she would know."

"That's likely," I said. "As Nathanial was the one to over-hear the conversation between Tessa and Miss Woods today."

"Another one I'll have to question," Sam said, sighing heavily. "Though from Tessa's actions, I really don't think it will be too hard to get a clear story from Miss Woods."

He smiled down at me, a rather pleased glimmer in his eye.

"Well done, Mrs. Lightholder. I'm impressed with your detective skills."

"Thank you, Inspector," I said.

"If you would be so kind as to walk back to the station with me, I can get a full statement from you for our records, and make sure that you get a chance to sit down once your nerves stop singing," he said.

"I would like that," I said. "Very much."

I did just that. I walked back to the station with him, helping him to put the rest of the pieces together. His eyes narrowed slightly when I told him about the way she was pursuing Mr. Fenton again, but I kept Tessa's comments about my relationship with him to myself. I didn't need to jeopardize anything between us with it.

I spent the rest of the afternoon at the station, filling out paperwork, getting examined by the local doctor, and reassuring everyone that I was, indeed, just fine.

All I wanted to do by the end of the day was just to excuse myself and go home for a rest.

Even though I was completely fine, realizing that Tessa would likely never have been able to kill me with that trowel like she wanted to, I was still exhausted.

That, and it was quite troubling to realize that she had killed Mrs. Lowell out of jealousy...which she freely admitted to Sam Graves, no more than five minutes into their questioning. Jealousy. Because she was infatuated with Mr. Fenton.

From her record, she would have likely moved past him eventually...and now, because of her actions, she would never get the chance to be with him.

Not that he would have ever wanted to be with her in the first place.

As I was leaving the station, I saw him walk into the building, a petrified look on his handsome face. My heart sank as I walked past him, knowing that the news of who killed Mrs. Lowell was going to devastate him, and it was going to be like losing her all over again.

I made my way home, grateful for the quiet and the peace that solving a case like this brought.

As I unlocked the door to my home, I realized this was the third time I had experienced a case like this. Three times I had learned dark truths. Three times innocent people had lost their lives as a result of others' selfishness.

It was hard to stomach, and so I set my thoughts on

enjoying a good book, perhaps a slice of Irene's apple crumb cake, and settling into a hot, sudsy bath.

I trudged up the stairs, my limbs heavy, my head buzzing. There was a soft ringing in my ears, and I couldn't quite shake it.

I flicked on the light upstairs, sighing with relief.

I found my teacup from breakfast that morning waiting on the dining table in the middle of the kitchen, the last few sips having lost their heat long ago. The ceramic jar where I kept the sugar cubes sat beside it, patiently waiting to be used once again.

The grey jacket I wore when it rained was draped over the back of one of the chairs, the sleeves stiff from drying in that position.

I let out another sigh, wandering back toward the bedroom. Food could wait. The bath, however, certainly could not.

I took one step into the sitting room, which was still somewhat dark...and something *crunched* beneath my feet.

I thought my heart would stop.

I looked down, and saw something glinting off the carpet.

The blood pounded in my ears as I slowly made my way to the lamp on the side table, and flicked on the light.

Little shards of glass glittered on the floor, perfectly still and wickedly sharp.

I looked around, wondering where on earth it had come from. A quick glance up at the window told me it wasn't from there. It wasn't from the mirror behind the sofa. And it wasn't from any of the vases or other breakable items around...

It was a moment before I wandered around the other

side of the coffee table...and found a picture frame over-turned, sitting atop some of the broken glass.

I stooped and picked it up, shaking some shards from it.

My heart sank when I saw it was the photograph of Roger and me.

I froze. This hadn't been broken this morning. And if it had simply fallen from its place on the credenza, it wouldn't have shattered across the room the way it had, or splintered the frame.

*It must have been thrown...*I thought, icy fear prickling my skin.

Did that mean...that someone had broken in...*again?*

Frightened, I stood, clutching the frame to my chest.

Why this photo? Why attack me in such an emotional way?

I did a quick search throughout the rest of the flat, and found nothing else out of sorts in the sitting and dining areas. Everything in the kitchen was fine, as well.

But as I stepped into the bedroom...I found something else amiss.

The shadowbox that I had collected all of Roger's letters into and hung on the wall near my bed was lying on the floor, broken open, my hairbrush lying beside it. More splintered glass was strewn about on the floor.

And the shadowbox was completely empty, all of the letters that I'd tucked inside missing.

My knees gave way beneath me, and I grabbed the wall as I slid down to the floor, my hands trembling.

The burglar wasn't after my belongings. Just like the last times, my jewelry was safe, my money was secure, and all of my inventory down in the shop was undisturbed.

Whoever it was that kept breaking into my home was after something to do with Roger.

My nerves sang as I looked down at the photo of Roger in my arms, and tears welled up in my eyes.

"What happened?" I asked him, his smiling face a reflection of much happier times in our life. "What do these people want with you?"

I looked away, knowing full well that he wouldn't answer me.

But answers were what I needed. Now more than ever.

The time had finally come to track this person down. I needed to find out exactly who it was that was continually breaking in and threatening my privacy the way they were.

It had to be someone who knew something about Roger that I didn't.

But why those letters? Why smash the picture of us? Was this person trying to send me a sign?

Did they want me to forget about him? Were they trying to warn me?

I would not get the answers I wanted just by sitting against the wall of my bedroom, nor were my tears going to fix my problems for me.

This was becoming a great deal more dangerous than I ever would have originally thought...and something told me that getting Sam involved in this again was not going to make things any easier.

This was something that only I could do.

I staggered up to my feet, wiping the tears out of my eyes.

"I will finish whatever you started, Roger. I will figure out why this person is doing what they're doing. I will put an end to it, and I will find a way to make peace with all of this, once and for all."

I pulled the photo of Roger out of the frame and walked back into the sitting room. I found a spare magnet on the refrigerator, and put the picture of Roger and I up there.

Then I glanced around the empty room. "Whoever you are, *wherever* you are, you haven't broken me. And you won't."

I meant it. I was going to finish this.

～

Continue following the mysterious adventures of Helen Lightholder in
"A Simple Country Tragedy."

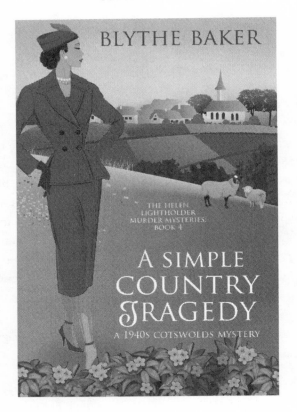

BLYTHE BAKER

THE HELEN
LIGHTHOLDER
MURDER MYSTERIES:
BOOK 4

A SIMPLE
COUNTRY
TRAGEDY
A 1940s COTSWOLDS MYSTERY

ABOUT THE AUTHOR

Blythe Baker is the lead writer behind several popular historical and paranormal mystery serieses. When Blythe isn't buried under clues, suspects, and motives, she's acting as chauffeur to her children and head groomer to her household of beloved pets. She enjoys walking her dog, lounging in her backyard hammock, and fiddling with graphic design. She also likes binge-watching mystery shows on TV.

To learn more about Blythe, visit her website and sign up for her newsletter at www.blythebaker.com

Made in the USA
Coppell, TX
24 February 2021

50804426R00092